stealing summer

THE BAYSIDE LAKE SERIES

JESS BRYSON

stealing *SUMMER*
THE PLAYLIST

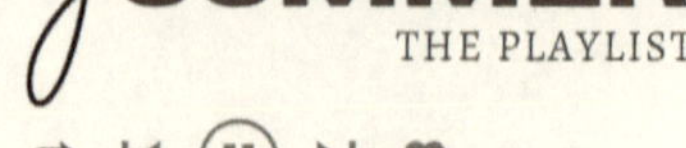

01.	**Rewrite the Stars** Michael Gerow	16.	**Two Hearts** Dermot Kennedy

01. **Rewrite the Stars**
Michael Gerow

02. **Cruel Summer**
Taylor Swift

03. **7 Summers**
Morgan Wallen

04. **Wildfire**
Nate Smith

05. **Guilty as Sin?**
Taylor Swift

06. **goodnight n go**
Ariana Grande

07. **Look What You Made Me Do**
Taylor Swift

08. **Wild Ones**
Jessie Murph & Jelly Roll

09. **we can't be friends**
Ariana Grande

10. **Water**
Tyla

11. **Illusion**
Dua Lipa

12.. **Delicate**
Taylor Swift

13. **Miss Summer**
Redferrin

14. **Truck Girl**
Josh Ross

15. **Snooze**
SZA

16. **Two Hearts**
Dermot Kennedy

17. **Still Yours**
The Kid LAROI

18. **Daylight**
Taylor Swift

19. **Just About Over You**
Priscilla Block

20. **Slow It Down**
Benson Boone

21. **Notice**
Thomas Rhett

22. **Regret in the Morning**
Conner Smith

23. **The Alchemy**
Taylor Swift

24. **making the bed**
Olivia Rodrigo

25. **numb**
Sam Tompkins

26. **Belong Together**
Mark Ambor

27. **When Im Gone**
LECADE

28. **Never Leave**
Bailey Zimmerman

29. **Where I want To Be**
Forest Blakk

30. **Blindsided**
Kelsey Balereni

HE SPUN THE BOTTLE, and my chance to escape was gone. As the bottle's momentum dwindled, so did my spirit, leaving my stomach tangled in knots. My breath was shallow. Each exhale was a silent plea—please, not me. I watched with wide eyes, willing it to pass by me. Just another inch, just a—

The collective gasp told me everything I needed to know before I even saw it.

"It's pointing right at her!" The girl next to me insisted, relieved, as she pointed a finger at me and inched her body in the opposite direction.

Of course, it landed on me. As if drawn by some cruel magnetic force, there it was, pointing accusingly, sealing my doom.

"Looks like it's your lucky day," Beau said, his voice flowing with a confidence he clearly didn't possess outside of this dark basement.

My gaze shifted from the condemning bottle to him, taking in his self-satisfied smirk. He licked his dry lips in a slow, deliberate motion, and I suppressed the urge to cringe. His hand raked through greasy hair that fell back into place as though completely untouched.

"Just do it already!" someone shouted, and the group formed a tighter circle as all eyes were on me and my impending embarrassment.

"Relax, you can't rush the magic," Beau said, as he leaned in closer, his scent of cool ranch chips mingled with the fall-scented candle flickering in the basement.

I squeezed my eyes shut so tightly I could see stars against the darkness of my eyelids. Beau was inches away, and every second felt like an eternity as I braced for the inevitable.

"What the fuck is going on down here? What are you, 12?" An unmistakable and irritating voice chastised.

When I snapped my eyes open, I saw that Beau's expression had morphed into one of surprised annoyance. A surge of relief coursed through me, and I was able to breathe again.

My brother, Parker, was standing at the foot of the stairs. Behind him were three of his baseball teammates—all of them in their team jackets, right behind him like an oppressive wall.

"Guess that means you're done playing, huh?" Beau leaned back, running his hand through his hair again, and this time there was no hiding the deflation in his posture.

"Oh, she's done playing alright." Boston, my brother's best friend, smirked as he watched Parker closely—clearly amused.

"If you touch my sister, I will unfortunately have to punch you in the face," Parker crossed his arms before he shot a death glare at Beau. "And trust me, you don't want that inconvenience tonight."

Beau's Adam's apple bobbed as he gulped, and color quickly drained from his cheeks. His hands rose up in surrender, a clear signal that the warning had hit home.

"Sorry," I whispered, backing away. "He doesn't always play well with others."

My eyes met Parker's for a split-second before I let out an exasperated sigh. "You're so annoying," I said, injecting a tone of irritation I was far from feeling. A slight smile betrayed my words, because, despite my annoyance at Parker, relief flooded through me.

Parker might be an overbearing brother at times, but tonight, I was thankful for that interruption.

I made my way to the stairs, following behind Parker, not daring to look back at the circle of faces or at Beau, whose moment of triumph had been so swiftly snatched away.

"Seriously, Chandler?" Parker scolded as we reached the top step. "I didn't bring you to this party so you could play with weirdos in the creepy ass basement."

"I ventured off, okay? Sometimes it's annoying listening to everyone with their, 'Awesome season, Parker!' or 'Boston, you're a legend!' I get it. You had a great season." I threw my hands up in the air, feeling the weight of their stares. "But that doesn't mean you two are gods or something."

"We don't ask for all the attention," Parker interrupted, his tone softening. "And you're right, we're not gods, but we sure are fucking legends." He smirked.

I pinched the bridge of my nose and shook my head, feeling the tension ease. "Whatever," I sighed.

"Let's get out of here," Parker urged, checking the time on his phone. "This place has a weird smell. You know how I am about smells."

"Fine. Just let me use the bathroom," I responded, already edging my way through the crowd toward the restroom. "I'll meet you out front."

"Make it quick!" he called after me, heading in the opposite direction.

As I stepped out of the front door a few minutes later, I pulled it shut with a gentle click and turned to find Parker lounging on the porch. He had that casual slouch he always did when he was making an effort to appear nonchalant. A half-smile played on his lips as if there was an inside joke he wasn't telling me about. Beside him, propped against the whitewashed railing, was Boston.

"Well, if it isn't the make-out queen herself," Parker teased, pushing off from the porch and shoving his hands into the pockets of his faded jeans.

"Shut up." I rolled my eyes, tucking a stray wave behind my ear. "And why are you both out here? I don't need security just to walk a couple of blocks," I asked, ignoring the way my heart skipped at the sight of Boston's ocean-blue eyes on me.

"We're heading back to our place after we walk you. And after that basement sitch, I'm not so sure about you," Parker glared at me playfully.

Truthfully, I was deeply relieved he interrupted—without him, I would still be in that basement and probably mortified. "Thanks for that save, by the way."

Parker slung an arm around my shoulders with a squeeze. "Anytime, sis."

Boston chimed in, his hands sliding into the pockets of his jacket. "So you excited for a summer in Bayside?"

I glanced up at him, and let out a playful sigh, falling into step between the two of them. "Oh yeah, super excited to be lazy and layout while you two do your baseball thing all summer," I responded, not revealing the fact that this would mean more time around Boston—and that wasn't a bad thing.

We made our way down the sidewalk until we arrived at my place. And then, as if on cue, the first firefly of the season twinkled in the darkness of the front yard.

"Hey look, fireflies are out," Boston said softly, his smile subsiding as I followed his gaze. His eyes reflected the tiny flashing light, and for a moment, I could see that familiar glint—the one that hinted at a memory only we shared.

"Summer's almost here," I murmured, more to myself than to them. The sight of that firefly didn't just signal the change of seasons; it ushered in a flood of memories, especially of how I first met Boston.

"Remember how we used to catch them in jars?" Parker asked, his voice tinged with nostalgia.

I nodded at Parker as I sat on the front steps, thinking about how I remembered it all too well. That night, fireflies danced through the warm summer air, their tiny lights flickering like stars that had magically fallen to Earth. It was a memory I held close—a memory of innocence and the very first time a boy had ever made my heart skip a beat.

* * *

As a wild five-year-old child, I was covered head to toe in dirt from my countless escapades. I relished the long summer days that seemed to never end. "Chandler, time to eat!" my mother's voice would call, and I'd rush inside to stuff my mouth full of food before darting back out to play.

That evening the neighborhood kids organized a competition of who could catch the most fireflies in glass jars, creating a luminous spectacle of captured wonder. I was determined to win and tried every tactic I could think of—jumping, running, and even holding my breath. I was convinced that stillness would make me invisible to the fireflies.

But victory was slipping away from me, and my frustration had begun to bubble into tears. Parker teased me mercilessly, and I couldn't stand losing to him. Just as despair threatened to overtake me, a hand larger than mine, and covered in dirt, reached out and swapped my near-empty jar for a brimming one.

I turned to see a boy, a stranger, whose bright eyes sparkled like the very fireflies he had collected. My heart raced as I met his gaze, and then, without a word, I slid a homemade friendship bracelet off my wrist and into his hand as a silent offering of thanks.

His smile was so friendly, so warm, it made the lingering stress from the possibility of losing to Parker melt away. I felt a connection in that moment—a bond formed over the simplicity of a summer's night. He continued his hunt for fireflies just before his mother's dinner call pulled him away and into the house next door. That was the first time I met Boston Riley.

As I laid in bed that night thinking about my glorious victory, the soft glow of the fireflies in the jar beside me painted my room in ethereal light. Little did I know this boy would become my first crush —a crush that would only grow stronger as he walked me home from school, let me win at every board game we played, and made me laugh until I couldn't breathe.

Later that week, Boston's mom invited our family over for dinner. Parker and Boston quickly became inseparable—a friendship that was fueled by their passion for sports. The three of us grew up together—building forts out of blankets and sharing secrets under the starlit sky, even though my parents forced Parker to include me most of the time.

"Come on, Parker, take your sister," I heard my mom's voice echo down the hallway, her tone non-negotiable. "She goes with you, or you don't go at all."

I peered around the corner as I clutched my raggedy doll to my chest and watched my older brother's face as it twisted into a scowl. My parent's rules and requests often annoyed Parker, especially when it came to his little sister tagging along.

"Fine," he grumbled, as he snatched up his baseball mitt from the kitchen counter. His eyes darted toward me, and I could almost see the internal eye-roll he suppressed.

I watched them practice their swings and throws in the back-yard, often feeling like a silent observer of some sacred ritual. Boston embodied perpetual summer—a cascade of brownish-blonde beach waves, glacial-blue eyes that promised endless joy, and a smile that could thaw the iciest of hearts.

As we got older, I started to notice the attention he would get from other girls—their admiring glances and flirtatious giggles. He drew them in effortlessly with his charm and sweet nature. I couldn't deny feeling a twinge of jealousy, but deep down I knew he was just being himself and it was impossible for anyone not to be drawn to him.

* * *

The first time I noticed, I sat by my open window, enjoying the cool breeze as I worked on my homework. The laughter outside had snapped my attention away from my textbook. Peering through the curtain, I caught sight of Audra Richwood, a girl with perfectly straight hair, standing by Boston's front porch.

"Hi, Boston! I made these and thought you might like them," she cooed, holding up a box tied with a red ribbon. Her giggles caused my eyes to roll to the back of my head. Boston, ever the gentleman, accepted the gift with a smile, his shoulders relaxed despite the blush forming on his cheek.

"Thanks, Audra. That's really sweet of you." His voice was a mix of gratitude and a hint of unease that only I could detect.

"Anything for you," she flirted back, stepping closer. Her intentions couldn't have been clearer.

I shook my head. The scene before me was a cliche straight out of a teen movie. I wondered if this was what high school was about. Baking for boys you like and awkward exchanges on the front porch.

"Goodnight, Boston," Audra's voice was lower now, promising things unsaid.

"Night, Audra." Boston stood there, holding the box like a question mark.

With a sigh, I let the sheer curtains fall back into place and shut my window, muting the world outside. My fingers found the volume button on my computer, giving it a push. The opening chords of a song filled the room, drowning out the reality of the boy next door becoming everyone else's dream. It was easier to lose myself in the music than to wonder why my heart felt heavy, why the thought of him with anyone else stirred a storm inside me.

* * *

"We were pretty good at catching fireflies, weren't we?" Boston's voice pulled me from my memories.

I laughed softly, though it sounded more wistful than I intended. "You were always better at it than me, Boston."

But as I glanced at him, I felt a pang of longing for a time when he wasn't so out of reach. Things were different now, and we didn't exactly run in the same social circle in college. I wasn't an athlete like he was. I spent most of my time with my roommate, Kristina, and a group of the theater students because the thrill of performing in front of an audience was something I couldn't get enough of, and we all understood it. Our group may have been small, but we could always count on each other—and that was all I needed. The idea of romance in real life was daunting and out of my comfort zone—I found solace in acting and playing out fictional love stories instead.

I stifled a yawn, the exhaustion finally catching up to me. "Thanks for walking me home, guys," I replied, as I pulled out my keys. "I'm sure I'll see you both around campus before we leave town."

"Alright, then. Sleep tight, Chandler," Parker said, his tone brotherly as ever.

"Night, Chandler," Boston said, shooting me a wink before pushing off from the railing.

two

I WAS ALMOST through my first year of college, but somehow surviving this final week of pointless classes felt more brutal than the entire year. I dragged myself out of bed, knowing that only a strong cup of coffee from the cafe could save me from the distress of this last school day.

"Chandler!" Parker's voice made me look up from my phone on my way out of the cafe, Boston right behind him with that calm smile that seemed to light up the campus.

"Hey," I greeted, tucking a loose strand of hair behind my ear, not expecting to run into either of them.

"Grabbing a coffee myself. Wait up a sec. We'll walk you to your class," Parker said, already edging past me without waiting for my reply.

"Sure," I responded, looking down at the time on my phone.

His absence left me acutely aware of being alone with Boston— all tall and effortlessly gorgeous. He leaned against the wall, glints of sunlight filtering through the tall windows catching him at just the right angles.

"Let me guess. You already took a selfie of your coffee and posted it on your story?" Boston teased, with a subtle lift of his brow.

"That's so lame. Who would do that?" I managed a weak smile before quickly deleting the last picture I posted on my story. "And it's not called a selfie unless it's a picture of yourself."

"I see," he observed, a playful tilt to his lips.

Then, out of nowhere, a girl brushed past, her hand lingering on Boston's arm just a second too long.

"Hey, Boston," she batted her long thick lashes. "Saw your last game. The way you made those outs at shortstop was so impressive." She winked; her flirtation was annoyingly obvious.

"Thanks," Boston replied. His voice held a note of polite distance that didn't stop my stomach from twisting.

"See you around," the girl said, throwing a wink over her shoulder as she walked away.

"Fans," he shrugged, turning back to me as if nothing had happened.

That girl's obsession with Boston forced back memories from high school. It was nothing new—I remembered moments like these like it was yesterday.

* * *

I blinked, unaware of my own expression until I saw it reflected at me in the mirror of my locker—a sharp glare, lips pursed in a scowl. Resting bitch face. I definitely needed to work on that.

"Chandler!" The voice came at me like a viper's strike, all sharp edges and hissing syllables. It was Amber Collins. Her expression pinched as she glanced nervously around before thrusting a folded piece of paper into my hand.

I could almost hear the strained screams of her scalp. Her slicked-back hair was snatched so tightly into a neat bun that it seemed as if any more tension would surely cut off the circulation to her brain. I wondered to myself if her over-styled 'do was an attempt to compensate for the absurdity of her shorts—frayed denim cut-offs with pockets that dangled below the hemline, larger than the shorts themselves.

"So, will you give it to him?" Amber demanded, her tone laced with impatience and something else—a desperate hope masquerading as disdain.

"Give it to who?" I said, playing dumb, knowing full well that the 'him' she was referring to could only be one person at school.

"To Boston," Amber snapped, her eyes darting toward the figure approaching from across the hall. The sight of Boston Riley always had a way of sending a ripple through the crowd. His tall, athletic frame moved toward us, his wavy hair catching the light, the piercing blue of his eyes scanning the hall until they landed in our direction.

"Sure, Amber. I'll give your note to Boston," I replied, the words sliding off my tongue with practiced ease, even though a part of me wanted to crumple the paper right there and toss it into the nearest trash can. "Although you do have the option of giving it to him yourself."

Why did everyone think I was their gateway to Boston Riley back then? I never signed up to be the go-between or the messenger for him.

"Thanks, Chandler. You're a lifesaver," Amber said, not quite able to keep the eagerness from her voice. She flashed a quick, insincere smile before turning on her heel and walking away with a sway that suggested she believed Boston's eyes were on her. They weren't.

Boston approached with a flicker of confusion crossing his features as he took in my bemused expression and the note I held between my fingers.

"You wrote me a love letter? You shouldn't have," he teased, flashing a grin.

"Not a chance!" I said while handing him the folded note, our fingers brushing briefly in the exchange. I was just the one who delivered them, apparently.

"Amber's work, I presume?" Boston quirked an eyebrow as he unfolded the note and scanned the contents with a casual curiosity.

"You would be correct." I leaned back against the wall, watching him with amusement. "You'd think they'd start getting more creative with their delivery methods." That was probably the fifth letter that month he got from a girl—at least the second from Amber.

Boston snickered as he looked up from the note, his gaze meeting mine. For a moment, we stood in silent understanding—both knowing it would be another letter that was going to end up in that little box he kept in his locker with the others. Boston was too nice to throw any of them out, but not interested enough to ever send one back.

"Let me guess... She thinks you're so dreamy, just like all the other girls at school." I said, crossing my arms.

"Do they now?" he said, biting his lip while giving me a lingering look before he put the combination code into his locker nearby.

"Seems like it," I shrugged, trying to shake off the intensity of his stare as I busied myself by shifting the bracelets on my wrist.

"And what do you think?" he said before tossing the letter inside the box and shutting his locker.

I opened my mouth to answer, but before I could form the words or even figure out what to say, Parker's voice interrupted, "Guys, you will not believe what just happened." He held his hands in the air for a dramatic effect.

My brother always had great timing, and he always left us smiling, even against our better judgment. Boston cocked an eyebrow, clearly curious. "What, did you finally walk down the hallway without tripping over your own feet?"

"Ha-ha, hilarious, but no." Parker leaned closer, lowering his voice as if sharing a secret. "I found lint in my belly button. Actual lint!" His expression was a mix of wonder and surprise, as if this minor discovery was the most astounding thing since sliced bread.

I couldn't help it. A laugh slipped out, the sound mingling with

Boston's deeper snicker. This was a typical Parker thing to say, always something ridiculous.

"Wait," I paused. "You're telling me you didn't know belly button lint was a real thing?"

Parker shrugged as he nodded earnestly. "Swear on baseball. I thought it was just something parents tell kids to make sure they wash themselves."

"Man, I thought you were better than this," Boston joked, slapping Parker on the back. "Basic hygiene, buddy. Basic hygiene."

They continued their usual horseplay in the hallway, and the moment was gone.

* * *

What did I think of Boston Riley? He had captured my heart from the moment I met him. He was the dreamy boy-next-door that inspired me to doodle his name in hearts all over my notebooks.

"Let's go before you're late," Parker said quickly, breaking me away from my thoughts.

When my excruciatingly long day was over, I had barely walked into my dorm room before she crashed into me. Her arms enveloped me in an embrace that I knew was both a hello and a goodbye. It was the kind of hug that spoke volumes without saying a word, the kind of hug that could only be from one person.

"Kristina," I laughed, squeezed tightly in her grip, "I can't breathe!"

"Sorry, sorry!" she said, pulling back just enough to let me catch my breath, but not enough to let go completely.

"Can you believe it?" she said, excitement lacing her words. "We survived our first year of college!"

Kristina was also a performing arts major, and we've grown really close over the past year.

"Not really. It flew by a lot quicker than I thought it would." I added, while taking off my backpack and placing it on my chair.

"Summer drama program, here I come." She sighed, slouching her shoulders.

"You're going to crush it," I grinned, feeling excited for her. Kristina was always ready to dive into lines and live out the emotions of any character. Being in the spotlight together was such an incredible feeling—we loved everything about theater.

Her smile faltered slightly. "I wish you were going with me," she whispered, sincerity soaking through her words. "I bet you're going to have the best summer though. I've heard Bayside is such a beautiful vacation spot. My cousins go boating there sometimes."

"Yeah, it's pretty," I shrugged. "I've been to a bunch of Parker's baseball games there, but this will be the first summer I'm staying."

"First time for everything, right?" Kristina nudged me playfully, before her expression softened. "Who knows what adventures you'll find yourself in? Maybe a summer romance? Maybe even with Boston?" She wiggled her eyebrows teasingly.

I laughed. "Oh, come on, Kristina. You know me better than that. I'll probably just end up reading and getting a sunburn."

"A long sigh escaped her lips. 'Well, I'm going to miss you."

"Don't worry, we'll be back here in no time," I assured her, although I secretly wished I could join her instead of being stuck with my brother all summer, who probably only asked me to come along because he felt sorry for me. My options were to tag along with Parker, or stay with my parents, and help mom with all her summer projects—which wasn't happening. "Besides, you better FaceTime or text me any chance you get."

"Promise." Her eyes held a hopeful glint. "Sweets to the sweet! Farewell," she stated firmly, with a soft smile. A line that always brought a smile to our faces from the last theater production we were both in.

three

SUMMER WAS FINALLY HERE, and with it, the promise of long, lazy days spent by the lake. I couldn't wait to leave the school year behind and feel the warm sun on my skin. But more than anything, I was excited about the baseball games.

I could already hear the crack of the bat, the cheers of the fans, and the smell of hot dogs and popcorn that blended together. And then there were the peanuts. There's something about that salty, slightly sweet flavor that just screams "baseball game."

I always made my brother think that going to his summer games was an inconvenience, rolling my eyes, sighing dramatically, and walking reluctantly toward the car with a sour attitude. Deep down, I loved everything about it, even sitting next to Mom and Dad, who were usually the loudest and most embarrassing ones in the crowd. There was nothing like watching Parker catch behind the plate—or Boston crushing a ball out of the park.

Parker drove, playing his stereo way too loud, for two whole hours. The eagerness built within me as we rounded a bend in the road, revealing the breathtaking panorama of Bayside Lake. My heart skipped a beat at the view—clear blue waters stretching to meet the horizon, framed by the lush forest and tall mountains in the distance.

"We're here!" Parker yelled, his excitement echoing my own as he pointed toward the small cabin nestled among the trees.

Our excitement was palpable as we tumbled out of the car, eager to finally get inside. The scent of families grilling out and the smell of fresh water and wet rocks filled the air.

Boston had already arrived and was taking his bags inside. He threw us a wave. His bright eyes caught mine for a moment too long, causing a familiar flutter in my stomach.

"Welcome to Grandpa's pride and joy," he said, sweeping an arm toward the cabin with a welcoming smile. "He left it to my mom, but you know she hates Bayside and doesn't want to deal with it. She has a friend who rents it out and manages it during the year though, so it's kept up."

Boston had another connection to this place other than baseball. His mom grew up in Bayside and raved about its beauty, but her memories were far from idyllic.

"Do you think she'll make it to any of the games?" Parker ventured gently, knowing the answer but asking anyway.

"Probably not," Boston sighed, his voice low. He glanced down at his hands, a sense of helplessness washing over him. "She has too much on her plate at work."

According to his mom, this town wasn't kind to her as a teenager. Cliques and mean girls had made school miserable, and she couldn't wait to leave it all behind. In recent years, Boston and Parker have taken advantage of the cabin being in Bayside, one of the most coveted spots for summer baseball in North Carolina.

"Maybe this summer will be different..." I began, although I knew I was giving him false hope.

"Maybe," he echoed, but we both knew the truth. The games would come and go, and Boston's heart would break a little each time the crowd cheered, and she was nowhere to be found. They were so close and she never missed a college game, but I've never seen her at any summer games.

Parker laid a comforting hand on Boston's shoulder, giving it a firm squeeze. "Bro, listen," he urged. Boston met his eyes, and Parker's gaze held nothing but conviction. "One day, when you go pro, you'll be able to take care of her. She won't have to work herself into the ground for much longer."

He nodded. I watched as the edges of my heart frayed a little. Boston was phenomenal on the field, but I could always tell in his face that he could never fully enjoy them without her watching.

"And don't you worry," Parker nudged him with a broad shoulder, his tone a mixture of concern and mischief. "I am going to make sure you have a very interesting summer."

"I don't doubt that for a second," Boston smiled, the tension in his shoulders easing ever so slightly.

"Well, it looks cozy," I pointed out, hoping my voice sounded steadier than I felt.

"I guess," Boston smiled, shoving his hands into the pockets of his jeans. "Your room is the first bedroom on the left when you pass the living room."

"Sounds good. I'm heading in to check it out," I announced as I pulled my luggage out of the car.

As soon as we got inside, Parker wandered over to the large bay window that looked out onto the shimmering lake.

"Home sweet home," he announced. "Look at some of these other houses around here, with their tennis courts and fancy boats tied up like they're trying to show off."

A lot of the local families who lived here were wealthy. Parker and I were by no means rich, more like middle-class. My mother worked as a teacher while my father worked in construction.

"Well, this cabin has charm," I challenged. "And enough room for us."

"Exactly," Parker replied, a softness entering his eyes. "Who needs a tennis court when you've got the whole lake?"

Natural light flowed through every inch of the cabin, and the cozy furniture and rustic decor seemed perfect for lazy days taking naps in front of the fireplace.

"I'm pretty sure I could sit out here all summer," Parker announced as he opened the screen door and claimed the first outdoor chair on the deck.

Soon, he and Boston were arguing over who would get the room that led to the patio, their grins mischievous as each argued their case. As I laughed watching them, it felt like the three of us were kids again.

Once they settled down, Boston leaned against the counter, and shot me that familiar smile of his. "I'll make us something to eat."

"You cook?" I blurted out in surprise.

"You know it's always just been my mom and me," he said, with a half-smile as he shrugged his shoulders. "Had to learn some skills to survive."

"Good to know," I grinned, happily surprised. "Because I'm nowhere near decent in the kitchen, and Parker... Well, let's just say he shouldn't quit baseball to be a chef."

From the patio drifted in Parker's voice. "Hey! I've been told the pizza rolls I make are superb, like no other!"

Boston gave me a sly glance, and we both stifled our laughter. "I'll take your word for it, bro!" he called back, shaking his head.

"Really, though," Parker's voice floated in with humor, "you don't know what you're missing. Culinary magic, I tell ya."

"You think he means tragic?" Boston whispered under his breath, earning him a playful shove from me.

"Well, maybe I can teach you a thing or two," he quipped, turning his attention to the sizzling pan before him. I didn't hate seeing him like this, showing a side of him that wasn't just about sports or the crowd he hung out with at school.

"Okay, chef," I said, playing along, "what do you need?"

"Grab some plates, will you?" He said as he turned off the stove.

I nodded as I opened the cupboard, reaching for the dishes. As we moved in the small space of the kitchen, laughter mingled with the clinking of plates. We sat down to eat, enjoying each other's company in this cozy cabin.

four

I MADE my way onto the wooden deck to lay out and get some sun. The planks were slightly heated under my feet from the midday rays. Boston cast another line into the lake and the lure plopped quietly into the still water.

"Think you'll actually catch something today?" I teased, stretching out on a nearby lounge chair, my eyes squinting against the brightness of the sun.

I wasn't mad about the possibility of having more of Boston's attention. He wasn't constantly surrounded by girls and friends like he would be at home.

"Oh, they're about to bite. Just you wait," he replied without looking back, his focus unfaltering.

"Uh-huh. I'm sure," I laughed softly, letting the sun bathe my face as I settled in and listened to the gentle lull of water against the dock, which was the most beautiful sound. "I could get used to this."

"Used to what? Me catching us dinner or you being lazy?" Boston responded, finally turning to flash me a smile. I could have easily spent my entire summer on this lounge chair just enjoying the view, and by view, I meant him.

"Definitely the second one," I shot back playfully.

Looking back, I caught sight of Parker ambling down from the cabin with a baseball mitt tucked under his arm. "You guys hear the news?" he asked eagerly.

Boston raised an eyebrow. "That you finally learned how to throw a curveball?"

Parker shoved him good-naturedly. "No, that we were assigned to the Blue Devils team this summer! Coach Ivy must've pulled some strings with the Blue Devils coach."

"No way!" Boston's face lit up. He turned to Parker, a grin spreading from ear to ear. "You know what this means? The Blue Devils—that's big. It's where the best of the best play the summer before they get drafted..."

"But wait, there's more," Parker said, holding up a hand. "You know this means we'll be on the same team as Reese."

Boston froze, eyebrows drawn together. "Shit. Reese Carrington."

Parker nodded. "One and only."

"Of course," Boston breathed. He raked a hand through his windswept hair, and I could see the competitive tension in his shoulders.

Reese Carrington was Boston's biggest rival. They had been on opposing teams every summer, cross-town rival teams. They were constantly compared by parents and coaches, though they were much different players with different positions. Boston was a shortstop and Reese, a pitcher who had expensive equipment and a cocky attitude to match his skills, which riled up Boston's competitive streak to no end.

It was a big deal when Boston stepped up to bat against Reese on the pitcher's mound. Reese and his team were notorious for their trash-talking, and allowing them to win was not an option. Two big fish in one small pond sounded like a recipe for disaster. But the potential outcomes for Parker and Boston outweighed all else.

"So what's the plan?" I asked Boston gently. "Your teammates now. You can't just avoid him all summer."

Boston's eyes flashed with determination. "I guess I'll have to focus on the game. If he still has an issue with me when we're on the same team, then that's on him."

I knew that look. This summer just got a lot more interesting.

I laid back and soaked up the bright sun as the two of them talked excitedly about the opportunity. This was no ordinary team—only the wealthiest families in town could afford for their sons to play on this elite summer squad, and I wasn't exactly sure how their college coach managed to get Boston and Parker on the team.

The next evening, we were summoned for our first Blue Devils event.

"Chandler! Over here!" My mom's voice stood out through the chatter, pulling my gaze to the left where my parents stood in excitement.

"Mom! Dad!" I called out, my eyes lit up as I spotted them standing next to a large sign that read 'Welcome Blue Devils Family!' in bold, friendly letters. The sign, adorned with blue and white balloons, stood tall, inviting us all to celebrate the shared passion that had brought many of us to this lakeside paradise.

My parents had made the drive from Stillwater, wearing the Blue Devils colors, looking every bit the proud supporters they were.

"Look at you three!" my mother exclaimed, her embrace encompassing both Parker and me before she turned to Boston, who had become an honorary member of our family. "And Boston, you've grown even taller if that's possible!"

Her words caused a sheepish smile to spread across his face. "Thanks, Mrs. H. It's good to see you," Boston responded warmly.

"We're so proud of you boys," my dad said, his voice rich with emotion as he clapped Parker and Boston on the back. "We can't wait to watch you this summer."

A large white tent was set up just outside the Blue Devils clubhouse. Under its billowing canopy were tables draped in sky-blue cloths, each with centerpieces showing the team's colors. The food stations offered everything from artisanal cheeses to tenderly grilled meats.

"Definitely not a backyard barbecue," I nudged Parker, my gaze roaming across the crowd.

"Grabbing a drink, then heading to the buffet," Dad yelled over his shoulder, motioning towards a server who was offering glasses of sparkling champagne.

"Hey, Mom, I'll be right back," I said, gently tapping her on the arm. "I want to use the bathroom and check out the clubhouse."

"Alright, darling." She offered a soft smile.

The door to the clubhouse gave a reluctant creak as I nudged it open, slipping inside, cautiously scanning the area to see if anyone was around. The room was still and silent. The walls were lined with gleaming trophies. I had known about the Blue Devils, but I never thought I'd be cheering them on.

My gaze drifted over the collection, pausing on a particularly impressive trophy that looked different from the others. It was a monument to breaking some sort of no-hitter record. The name etched onto the metal plaque beneath it caught my eye: Reese Carrington. I couldn't help but let my fingers trace the cold, embossed letters.

A smooth, calm voice broke through the silence. "You couldn't pay me to put that giant ass trophy on my wall."

Startled, I spun around—a gasp escaped my lips. Leaning against the dimly lit wall was someone who took my breath away—his posture was effortless and confident. A shiny pendant hung around his neck that caught my attention for a moment before I took him in. He was the kind of handsome that nearly rendered me speechless. It wasn't just his striking appearance, but it was those bright green eyes that were a stark contrast to his dark features. They sparkled with a mischievous glint that was both alluring and intimidating, making it almost unbearable to tear my gaze away.

"I agree," I managed, trying to keep my voice level, despite the way his eyes seemed to make me feel. "Anything associated with the name Reese Carrington seems to be... overcompensated."

"Overcompensated?" he echoed, raising an eyebrow as amusement flickered across his face.

"Definitely. I've heard his ego needs its own private island," I shrugged, mostly just trying to make conversation.

"Sounds like you're not a fan," he quipped, crossing his arms over his chest, and the motion drew attention to the way his shirt stretched across his well-defined muscles.

"Clearly," I replied, trying to sound unimpressed.

"Then I guess you've been warned." he pushed away from the wall, a shadow of a grin playing on his lips. "Stay away from that one."

"You don't have to tell me twice," I smiled, then tucked a strand of hair behind my ear.

"Well, I should get back," he said, his voice echoing slightly in the empty hallway of the clubhouse as he tilted his head toward the door. "See you around."

Without another word, he slipped out of the exit. And just like that, he was gone, leaving me standing alone, my thoughts a jumbled mess of curiosity—wondering who the heck that was and why my heart was still beating so fast.

I slid into the seat next to Mom as I checked my phone, wondering how Kristina was doing—but there were no alerts and nothing from her.

"Still no word?" Mom asked as she sipped on her iced tea.

I shook my head, trying to keep the frown at bay. "Nope. Nothing yet. But she's probably busy. She said it was a pretty intensive program."

"Sometimes it's good to disconnect and enjoy the moment," Mom offered with a reassuring smile.

"True. I just hope she's enjoying it." I managed a weak smile.

"I'm sure she will text you as soon as she can." Mom gave my hand a comforting squeeze.

I noticed a girl sitting alone at a table nearby watching the festivities, with a hint of boredom in her eyes. Her curly blonde hair was full of volume, and her energy radiated a sense of approach-ability.

Intrigued, I made my way over to her and introduced myself. "Hi there, I'm Chandler Hartford," I greeted her, trying to sound as friendly as I could.

She looked up at me slightly; her smile was warm and welcoming. "Willow, the coach's daughter and underpaid assistant. Nice to meet you."

We started a conversation easily and effortlessly—realizing how much we had in common. Willow's laughter was infectious, and I was drawn to her stories and how much knowledge and passion she had about the game. There was an instant connection—a sense of kinship that felt like reuniting with an old friend.

Just as we began to exchange phone numbers, the sharp clink against glass silenced us. We turned toward the sound, and it was the Coach, ready to make an announcement.

"May I have your attention, please?" His voice boomed through the gathering as conversations dwindled into silence. "I'd like to take a moment to welcome back all our returning families and extend a warm welcome to the new ones joining our team this year. I have high expectations of these boys and we're going to have a great season."

"Let's play some ball!" Coach Levy exclaimed, a twinkle in his eye that suggested he was as excited for the season. Then, with a slight shift of his stance, he gestured toward the back. "Now, let's hear a few words from last season's MVP. Come on up, son!"

The energy shifted, becoming electric as all eyes turned to the back. I glanced over and my pulse quickened as I tried to place who it was. Cheers erupted, whistles and howls pierced the air. The guy I had just been talking to in the clubhouse earlier rose from his seat and made his way toward the coach. His presence seemed to capture the attention of every eye in the area.

"Who is that?" I leaned over to whisper to Willow, still not taking my eyes off of him.

Willow smiled, her eyes sparkling. "Oh, I see someone is caught in his spell already—That's Reese Carrington, our starting pitcher, and a fellow local like myself."

Reese Carrington? Shit. My stomach plummeted, embarrassment and disbelief tangled in a sickening knot. Moments like these have to be the reason phrases like 'died of embarrassment' are a thing.

The coach patted him on the back and shook his hand with a proud expression.

I guess I never paid close attention to what he looked like when we played against him, but he was taller than I had remembered. His backward hat that he didn't have on earlier sat above his short, messy dark hair.

"We're taking it to the championship this year, baby!" he declared, his smile now fully cocky—not a hint of hesitation.

The response was immediate. Cheers detonated through the air, and his teammates roared his name—the name I was bashing earlier.

Teammates and others quickly swarmed around him, and the chatter resumed once again.

I paused, still in shock before I whispered to Willow, "I don't remember him looking like that last summer." My gaze was drawn back to Reese like a magnet. "He's insanely attractive. When did that happen?"

"I know, right?" Willow giggled. "He filled out real nice this past year. His fastball is also about 93 miles per hour."

"Does he play college baseball?" I asked, curious to know.

"Oh, yeah. He's at Duke. It's like a 30-minute drive from here. And Dad said he's definitely going pro if he can stay out of trouble."

"Trouble?" I echoed, arching an eyebrow, even though the concept didn't surprise me.

"Yeah," Willow nodded emphatically, her gaze fixed on him. "Every time I hear about some scuffle here at Bayside or even occasionally on the field, he's always right in the middle of it. He's always been nice to me but it's like he attracts chaos."

Reese worked the crowd, smug as ever, with an infuriating smirk plastered on his face. His confidence was hard to ignore. He went around shaking hands and clapping the other players on the back, laughing and joking, like he owned the place.

When he got to Parker and Boston, who were close by, he grinned and said, "Well, well, if it isn't the dynamic duo. I see they're letting just about anyone on the team these days."

Boston tensed, jaw clenched, but Parker just laughed it off and shook Reese's hand. "Good to see you too, Reese," he said pleasantly.

After Reese made his way through the crowd, he glanced over, flashing me a cocky grin that made me want to hide underneath the table. Maybe he'll forget about what I said? He probably gets it all the time—or maybe I should crawl into a hole to live out the rest of my days.

But still, that cocky grin somehow made my pulse race— followed swiftly by a pang of guilt. What was I even doing admiring Reese like this? I didn't even know him. It was also alarming that Boston had never had a problem with anyone, except Reese—which meant he had to be bad news. But... it didn't hurt just to have eye candy, right? Reese may be the biggest jerk according to Boston and Parker, but that doesn't have to stop me from appreciating his good looks.

"He's having a party at his parents' lake house later tonight if you want to go," Willow said with a mischievous smile. My cheeks felt hot as I glanced at her.

"What party are we crashing?" Boston said, an amused expression playing across his face as he and Parker took a seat next to me at the table.

I glanced back and forth between Boston and Willow, unsure of how to respond, knowing he wouldn't like the answer.

Willow's eyes sparkled as she exchanged a glance with Boston. "Reese is having a party tonight. First one of the season."

"I've heard stories about his parties," Parker said with awe.

Scowling, Boston shook his head. "Sounds like torture."

"Come on, don't be like that," Parker said, clapping him on the back. "Reese might be a jerk, but I've heard his parties are epic. Just look at it as a team bonding experience before we start the season."

"Willow, meet Boston and unfortunately, my brother Parker," I said, with a hint of annoyance.

Parker grinned widely, rocking back in his chair and injecting his unwanted charm into the conversation. "If this beautiful lady is going, we have to go."

Willow chuckled, a bit of sarcasm in her voice. "Of course, it wouldn't be a party without the coach's daughter."

"You're coach Levy's daughter?" Parker asked, his eyes widened in surprise.

"One of three, but definitely his favorite," she replied, winking at Parker.

Willow and I exchanged grins, already plotting our plan for the night. Parker's enthusiasm spilled over, and soon even Boston lightened up to the idea. I found myself swept up in the collective enthusiasm, momentarily forgetting about that embarrassing moment earlier.

five

BOSTON PULLED a t-shirt over his head, his damp hair sticking up at odd angles. He ran a hand through it, catching my eye in the mirror.

"You look nice," he said with a crooked smile.

I decided on my favorite black crop top and dark-wash jeans. I usually felt confident in this combo, but at that moment, I felt strangely self-conscious.

"Thanks," I mumbled, smoothing imaginary wrinkles from my top.

I heard the honk of Willow's car and we headed out to the front where her red convertible idled in the driveway. Parker strode ahead of me, calling out shotgun as Boston shut the door behind me.

"There they are! Hop on in." Willow greeted us cheerily as we climbed into the backseat. Her blonde curls bounced with enthusiasm.

Parker slid into the passenger seat beside her, and she put the car in motion. "Hope you don't mind me taking the front seat. Figured I'd give you the chance to put the moves on me," his voice lowering an octave. Even from the back seat, I could see the hint of a smirk playing on his lips.

Willow laughed lightly as her eyes flickered to meet his before returning to the road. "Keep dreaming, Peter."

The momentary glare that flickered across Parker's face quickly dissolved into another smile, this one more genuine and warm than the last. "It's Parker," he corrected. "…But I like that you have a nickname for me already," he winked.

I rolled my eyes at my brother's obvious flirtation, but my annoyance started to fade as we made our way down the dark, winding roads.

We pulled up at a large lake house. Its sleek and modern design stood out from the surrounding homes. Every detail seemed like it was brand new and custom, from the large glass windows to the unique angles of the roof. Cars flooded the driveway and l tried to look inside the glass windows, but the tint was too dark. We made our way to the front, where we could hear the music thumping and giggling from inside. I took a deep breath as we walked through the front door, allowing Willow to lead the way.

Parker and Boston were instantly swarmed by a group of baseball players. "My guys, glad you could make it!" One of the players said as the group merged into the party. I smiled, watching them seamlessly blend into the crowd.

The air was thick with the smell of cheap beer and cologne. Boys in baseball caps and athletic wear crowded the room, red solo cups in hand. A couple of players I recognized from earlier danced in the center, laughing as they moved to the music.

A few feet away, I spotted Reese, surrounded by a group of people. His presence commanded the room, and my eyes were drawn to him like a moth to a flame. Then someone made him laugh—and smile a genuine smile that I hadn't seen from him yet. His smile felt warmly comforting as the dimples in his cheeks deepened.

But then I noticed a few girls making their way over to me and Willow. Their eyes were bright with curiosity as they approached.

Willow placed a gentle hand on my arm. "Don't let them rattle you, love. That's just Caroline, she's the blonde in the middle and those are her friends—she kinda leads and the others follow. They're harmless, really, just eager for any gossip or news they can spread around."

I raised an eyebrow. "What could they possibly want to gossip about with me?"

"Boys and the Bayside Ball, of course," Willow said, a smile playing on her lips. "It's the event of the summer around here where they announce the MVP and all the awards at the end of the season for the Blue Devils. It used to be a regular award ceremony but I think the parents wanted an excuse to throw a huge party and now it's a big thing—they go all out."

I laughed. "Let me guess. It's also an excuse for everyone to get dressed in expensive outfits and be seen?"

Willow nodded. "You got it. Caroline and her friends are desperate to be asked by one of the baseball boys, and I'm sure Parker and Boston are on their radar. And you've been spotted with both. In their minds, a date to the Bayside Ball is a status symbol."

I shook my head, watching the girls approach, their dresses swishing around their knees. "Well, they're going to be disappointed. I don't have any insider information to share."

I took a deep breath as the girls surrounded us, bracing myself for the incoming questions.

"Hi there Sweet Pea! You're Parker's little sister, right?" said a girl with short, stylish brown hair while the others near her listened closely.

"Yes, unfortunately." I sighed.

The girls exchanged glances, and I could sense their curiosity. "Is he single? And what about Boston? We need all the scoop on him," asked Caroline, her eyes sparkling with mischief.

"Yes, Parker is single. And Boston, there isn't much scoop to tell. He grew up next door to us and now he lives with Parker and two of their teammates back in Stillwater. He's always lived and breathed baseball," I said, trying to sound nonchalant.

"So he's single then too?" asked one of the girls, watching me closely.

"He is," I said softly.

"So, nothing is going on between you and Boston?" Caroline leaned in close, her eyes wide with disbelief as she watched him across the room, still laughing with Parker and a few of their teammates. "I mean, look at him. He's so hot. And you grew up together. There must be some sort of history there."

I followed her gaze, feeling a tightness in my chest. History? You could say that again. He was the most perfect boy I had ever known, who happened to be attached at the hip to my brother. I adored him and pretended he was my prince charming for as far back as I could remember, but my heart sank knowing he'd never see me in the same way.

"Definitely history, but nothing to spill," I sighed, shaking my head to dispel the remnants of the past. "We grew up together, and he's my brother's best friend, that's all."

But that wasn't all. He wasn't so distant until high school happened, I thought, as I watched Boston wipe his brow with the back of his hand. He got popular, surrounded by pretty girls and athletes. And I... I found my comfort in the drama club and stage lights. We were in very different worlds now, and it didn't seem possible for them to collide. Boston was still Boston, effortlessly charming and impossibly out of reach. And I was still me, more comfortable reciting lines than living out a real-life romance.

Time seemed to stand still as I continued to listen to Caroline try to make small talk, and soon I found myself exchanging glances with Reese across the room. His eyes held mine for a few moments before I looked away, my cheeks flushed with heat. He was leaning casually against the marble fireplace mantel, holding a red solo cup. I couldn't stop myself from admiring how unfairly hot he was, then instantly wanted to kick myself for thinking so.

Willow noticed me glancing in his direction before I could look away. "C'mon, I see Reese over there. I'll introduce you," she said, linking her arm through mine and leading me through the crowd.

"Willow, I don't think this is a good idea," I panicked, dredging my heels into the polished wood floor, each step toward him amplifying my dread.

"Oh, it'll be fine," she said in a dismissive tone. She tugged me forward, her enthusiasm undiminished by my resistance.

"Reese, I'd like you to meet my friend Chandler," Willow said cheerfully.

Then he looked at me, taking me in completely, and the corner of his mouth twisted into a smirk that could only be described as devilish. "Oh, if it isn't my biggest fan."

Heat crept up my neck, painting my cheeks a mortified shade of red. "Yeah, sorry about that," I managed to say, forcing a smile that felt as shaky as my voice.

I glanced around, desperate for any lifeline to cling to, as Willow was now talking to his friend. "But you do have a beautiful home," I offered a smile, hoping it would be enough to smooth over the comments I made about him earlier.

Reese's reaction was minimal, his eyes holding mine for a mere moment before he acknowledged the compliment with a nonchalant, "Thanks." Then he took a sip from the cup he was holding before saying, "Enjoy the party."

Then, without another word, he finished the rest of his drink as he tipped it back in one smooth motion. His gaze drifted past me, scanning the room as if he were searching for something—or someone—far more interesting than me. His unjustified sense of entitlement was highly infuriating.

With ease, Reese set his empty cup down on a nearby table and turned his back to me, his shoulders broad and dismissive. The finality of the gesture left me standing there, feeling both slighted and oddly unsettled.

This was Reese Carrington—I knew about his arrogance on the field, his snide comments off it, and the way he seemed to revel in being a perpetual pain in the ass of anyone who crossed his path. Why did I even care?

I bit my tongue as irritation flared up inside me before redirecting my attention to Willow. "Well, he seems charming," I said sarcastically.

"Oh, don't let him get to you," Willow pleaded. "He's usually really nice. He probably just has a lot going on."

"Yeah, I can see that," I said, my voice dripping with disdain.

A sudden grip on my wrist pulled me away from Willow. I whipped around, strands of my hair catching in the draft, to find Parker's concerned eyes boring into mine.

"Why were you talking to Reese?" His voice was low and urgent.

"Maybe because it's his house," I said with a shrug, pulling away my wrist from his firm hold, "And Willow introduced me. It was the polite thing to do."

Parker's frown deepened as his gaze shifted momentarily toward where Reese stood. He leaned in, his voice a conspiratorial whisper. "Look, I know we're at his house, but do your best to stay away from him, okay? That is not the company you wanna keep."

"Really?" I countered with a firm glare. "And here I thought this was just a friendly social gathering."

His eyes narrowed slightly, the protective older brother mode kicking in full swing. "I'm serious, Chandler. You don't know him like we do. Reese has a reputation—"

"Trust me. I know all about the history—I've been to many games you've played against him, remember?" I pointed out, rolling my eyes for effect. "And you're not the company I wanna keep either, but here we are."

"Ha," Parker chuckled dryly, the corners of his mouth lifting into a forced smile. "Hey, I just know guys, and that is definitely not one I'd trust."

"Good thing I'm not asking you to trust him then," I retorted, already turning on my heel, ready to leave the conversation and irrelevancy behind. "Goodbye, Parker," I ended the conversation, my steps carrying me back toward Willow.

Willow was talking to another new face, and we were still in clear sight of Reese as he continued casual conversation with his friends. That crooked smile, those striking eyes—he was magnetic. Then... I saw her. A leggy brunette cozied up next to him, placing a perfectly manicured hand on his arm. She was gorgeous, of course. With her cascading dark locks and full lips, she looked like a model. The kind with a fierce glam squad. "Hey you," he said, pulling her into an embrace. "I was wondering when you'd show up."

My stomach twisted into knots. So this was his girlfriend. This was probably who he was searching for in the crowd. I couldn't deny the feeling of slight disappointment, even though I couldn't pinpoint why.

"Who's that with Reese?" I asked Willow, trying to sound casual.

"Oh, that's Blair Cassidy," Willow replied knowingly. "Her and Reese have been on and off forever. Looks like they must be on at the moment. Their dads both own the law firm in town. Those are two lawyers you don't want on your bad side."

I nodded, watching Blair whisper something in Reese's ear that made him laugh. They really did seem perfect together. Two ridiculously good-looking rich kids. I suddenly felt very out of place at this party. With a sigh, I turned away from Reese and Blair's intimate exchange with the image seared into my mind.

six

I MADE my way over to the crowded keg, hoping a refill would take my mind off Reese. I waited impatiently in the long line, shifting my weight from one foot to the other, checking the time on my phone again. It was 15 minutes before the line started creeping forward. When it was finally my turn, I struggled to work the tap, and it slipped from my grip, thudding to the floor. Foam spewed up as I scrambled, dropping my empty cup. It rolled away in the process while I cussed under my breath. Before I could get a handle on the tap, a pair of rough, powerful hands grabbed the other end.

"Here, let me help with that," a smooth voice said.

I glanced over to see Reese, with an amused smile playing on his lips. He stole an empty cup from the next person in line behind me and expertly filled it to the brim with beer before he handed it over.

"Thanks," I said, a bit flustered. Up close, his green eyes were even more mesmerizing.

"So, enjoying the party?" he asked, leaning against the wall beside us.

"Yeah, it's... lively," I said. An understatement, given the pulsing music coming from the other room, drunken laughter, and the couple currently making out on the couch nearby.

Reese lifted his chin. "Lively. I like that."

I smiled hesitantly, unsure what to make of his sudden friendly demeanor.

"So, your brother Parker's going to be my new catcher this summer," he said casually, while taking a sip of his drink.

I blinked in surprise. "How did you know Parker was my brother?"

"I asked around. I wanted to get all the details about my teammates," he shrugged, putting a hand in his pocket. "Seems like he's got a cannon for an arm. I like that in a catcher... Didn't realize he had such a cute sister though." His eyes trailed down my body.

My cheeks grew warm at the unexpected compliment, but I kept my expression neutral and glanced away while taking a sip of my drink. He was just trying to make conversation, I told myself.

"Whatever guy left you alone at this party must be crazy," he added, his voice lower now.

No, he wasn't making conversation. He was definitely flirting. Was he seriously trying to flirt after basically ignoring me earlier? I scoffed. "What makes you think there's a guy? Maybe I came alone."

"A girl like you?" One corner of his mouth quirked up flirtatiously. "Not a chance."

I bit my lip, unsure how to respond. Reese's confidence irritated me, no doubt about it. But the way he just looked at me made my heart race faster than I cared to admit.

"If you say so," I said dryly.

"Come on, lighten up," he urged. "It's a compliment."

I opened my mouth to respond, but suddenly Blair appeared at Reese's side, slipping her arm through his. "There you are! I've been looking all over," she flashed me a tight smile before turning to Reese. "Ready to take a shot with me, babe?"

Reese glanced between us, an eyebrow raised. "Yeah. See you around, Hartford." With a wink, he allowed Blair to lead him away, her grip possessive on his arm.

I stared after them, my heart pounding against my ribs. What just happened? And the way he looked at me... Shaking my head, I turned and hurried off in the opposite direction. Was he just trying to be friendly now, and that was his way of showing it?

Willow made the rounds, introducing me to various people at the party. Their names seemed to slip from my memory as soon as I heard them. Eventually, I walked outside to the backyard where Parker and Boston were deep into an intense beer pong game. They had been at it for a while, going shot for shot on five cups in a triangle formation.

"Come on, Boston! Make the shot!" A teammate cheered enthusiastically as he jumped up and down. Caroline and her friends hollered, egging the boys on. I took my phone out to distract myself. Their shrieking was closing in on my last nerve.

I took a seat on the pool deck while Parker and Boston continued to play best-out-of-five. The flickering lights from the tiki torches were casting shadows on the water's surface, and laughter resonated through the air. After a while, the wind started to pick up, blowing my hair into my eyes, so I used one hand to push it back. Hugging my arms around myself, I tried to ward off the chill that clung to my skin.

"You look cold. You want my hoodie?" Reese's voice came from behind me, startling me out of my thoughts. I turned to find him standing there with his signature smirk, his eyes bright with amusement.

Then, he effortlessly shrugged off his sweatshirt, which seemed too easy for someone his size. The fabric slid up as he pulled the garment over his head, revealing a glimpse of what was underneath —his abs teasingly made an appearance, taunting me.

"Thanks, but no thanks," I said, trying to sound indifferent. "I'm fine."

"Suit yourself," he nonchalantly placed the hoodie beside me on the deck just in case I changed my mind. Then he sat down next to me, leaving only a whisper of space between us. "You really don't like me, do you?"

"Is that so hard to believe?" I tried to keep my gaze focused on the beer pong game instead of his intense stare. "You haven't exactly been a saint when it comes to Boston and Parker."

* * *

My thoughts drifted back to last summer. My phone had buzzed relentlessly in my pocket then, Parker's name flashed on the screen.

"We're gonna need a little help," he huffed, sounding embarrassed about the words that were about to come out of his mouth. "Reese and his entourage pulled a prank—they swiped all our clothes from the locker room."

"Wait, what?" I remembered asking him, unable to stifle my own chuckle. "All of them?"

"Every. Single. One." Parker sighed. "Boston's fuming, and dude, we've got nothing but our gloves and cleats!"

That mental image had me biting my lip to keep from laughing out loud. Imagining them in this predicament was both startling and oddly satisfying. It was uncalled for and cruel, but I knew that since we were still in the area from the game, they had us to bail them out of this unfortunate predicament.

"Are you serious?" I managed, wondering how Reese even pulled this off.

"Dead serious. They snatched everything when we were in the shower. The rest of the team left already."

"Alright, Mom and I are coming," I'd said, shaking my head as I quickly threw away the meal I was eating. But nothing had prepared me for the sight that greeted me at the front doors of the recreation facility.

Boston stood there, completely exposed by his lack of attire. He wore a scowl that clashed with his usually cheerful nature, and then I noticed it—a baseball glove was clutched strategically over his nether regions. It was so absurdly comical that I couldn't help it—I snickered.

"Laugh it up," Boston grumbled, his cheeks tinted with the slightest hint of pink, betraying his embarrassment even as he tried to maintain his dignity. "Just wait till I get my hands on Reese."

"Hey, this is a good look on you," I teased, tossing him the gym bag filled with spare clothes that Mom had fortunately brought along. He smiled and rolled his stormy eyes.

"Thanks, Chandler," he said, his voice softening. "We owe you one."

* * *

"Fair enough," Reese agreed, leaning back on his elbows, looking completely at ease. "But people can change, can't they?"

"Maybe," I admitted, my thoughts reeling as I tried to determine what his angle was. "But not without good reason."

"Maybe you should make up your own mind about me. I could be different from what you think," he said, turning to face me, all traces of cockiness gone from his voice.

"I guess so... but," I hesitated, searching for the words to explain my reluctance before turning to look at him. "From what I've seen and heard, it seems like you're a jerk and you weren't too friendly when we met earlier."

A beer pong ball bounced off the table and rolled to a stop by my foot. Reese reached down, picked it up, and held it between his fingers. His eyes never left mine.

"Maybe I wasn't the friendliest earlier," he admitted, twirling the ball in his hand. "But then again, you said I was overcompensated. That's a pretty bold statement for someone who barely knows me."

"Is that your way of asking me to take it back?" I asked, allowing a half-smile to form, knowing that my comment may have struck even the faintest of a nerve.

"Let's call it an invitation to reconsider," he suggested, tossing the ball back toward the beer pong table without looking. It landed in a cup, causing a small cheer to erupt from the group. "Can we be even?"

"Even?" I echoed, as I pretended to consider. His charm was like a current, trying to pull me under, but I remained afloat, skeptical yet intrigued. "Fine," The word escaped before I even had a chance to think about it. "We're even."

Reese looked down, biting his lip as if contemplating something. His hand reached out, gently touching my chin and tilting it upward until our eyes met. He leaned in closer, his voice a seductive whisper. "I may be a jerk, but I'm good at other things, you know," he said huskily. "Go ahead, kiss me, and find out for yourself."

I couldn't help but laugh out loud at the audacity of his words. It was no secret that he was someone I should probably stay away from, but there was something about Reese's boldness that made it impossible not to be intrigued by him.

"You're unbelievable," I said, shaking my head. "Do girls actually fall for this charm of yours?"

"They do," Reese replied confidently, his eyes never leaving mine. "And it's just a matter of time before you come around, too."

I let out an uncontrollable laugh. Reese's smirk faltered briefly and he seemed a little hurt by my reaction, but soon enough, he couldn't help but smile.

"Is that so?" I teased after the laughter subsided, still grinning from ear to ear. "Well, I think it might take a bit more than a few smooth lines to change my mind about you. Like, maybe you being nice to my brother and Boston this season."

Reese grinned. "I'll keep that in mind. I'm cool with your brother —he's been guilty by association, but Boston I'll have to think about... Anyway, I better get back to the party but put my sweatshirt on. I know you're cold. It gets a little windy sometimes at night since we're so close to the lake."

"Bye, Reese," I whispered softly, watching as he walked away. There was no doubt about it this time, he was flirting with me. The interaction left me with a strange sensation—butterflies and guilt. I knew I couldn't entertain it. He had a girlfriend, and it was Reese. But still, there was an unexplainable sense of ease and familiarity in his presence. What was it about this infuriating boy that made it so difficult for me to ignore? And why did a part of me secretly hope he would succeed in winning me over?

Reese walked away and I couldn't shake the feeling of being watched. It was Boston and Parker—their eyes both locked on me and narrowed—which only added to the guilt gnawing at me.

The buzz I heard was subtle but interrupted the awkward moment, only to realize I'd missed Kristina's call during my conversation with Reese. A soft groan escaped my lips as I tapped the voicemail icon and brought the device to my ear.

"Hey, it's me," Kristina's voice crackled through with a blend of excitement and frustration. "I had such a long day but wanted to catch up. I've got loads to tell you! Why aren't you picking up?"

I could almost see her animated gestures, the way her eyes would light up with excitement. My heart warmed at the thought of her enthusiasm, even as I felt a twinge of guilt for not answering her when she called.

"Met this guy I'll be rehearsing with," she continued, her words picking up speed. "Oh, and he is really cute. Learning heaps already. I'm going to bed but can't wait to share everything with you—"

I felt a familiarity at the mention of this cute new boy, and I couldn't resist taking another peek at Reese, who was engaged in conversation with a group of people, before glancing back at Boston, who was watching me with an unreadable expression.

"Anyway, gonna try to catch you again soon," Kristina's voice pulled me back, "Love you!"

"Love you too," I whispered to no one, the screen already darkening as the voicemail ended.

As we got back into Willow's car to head home, Parker shot me a death glare like the sweatshirt I had on was more than inconvenient for him. "Seriously, Chandler?" he whispered. His voice was low but barely hid the disappointment. "Not cool."

"It's not a big deal—" I huffed.

On the way home, Boston didn't say much. I knew he was probably annoyed that I was wearing Reese's sweatshirt, but he never brought it up—he didn't need to. As he headed to my room, he flashed me a half-smile, but the moment had an uncomfortable edge that left me feeling uneasy.

Just after I slid into bed, restless fingers found my phone. With little thought, I began searching for Reese on Instagram. "Baseball, of course," I whispered to myself, as I continued to scroll through his Instagram feed where action shots of him on the field began to populate. And then, there it was—a photo that made me pause a little too long. Reese, shirtless by the lake. "Definitely a thirst trap," I whispered, chastising myself for lingering.

My thumb had already betrayed me, swiping to the next photo— a series of pictures with Blair. They looked like a picture-perfect couple from a magazine, always smiling and taking photos together at gatherings or on ski trips, and family events.

I found myself scrolling further and deeper until I landed on Blair's Instagram. Blair was stunning in every photo—whether she had make-up on, or was just lounging around in sweats. She had that natural glowing skin beauty, too.

"Okay, I need to stop," I whispered, as a few more rows of photos populated. And then, a catastrophic disaster struck in the form of a heart icon, suddenly glowing red beneath a photo from 2012. It was an innocent picture of her dog, a bulldog with a lopsided smile that almost seemed to mock me from the screen.

"Shit!" The word escaped my lips before I could fix the situation. "Undo, undo, undo!" I screamed, tapping furiously on the screen, hoping that the notification would somehow vanish into the air before Blair ever laid eyes on it. The un-hearted image stared back at me, making me realize that I needed to go straight to bed.

With a long sigh, I locked my phone, and the light extinguished along with the images. I went to sleep wearing Reese's sweatshirt, inhaling his scent—comforted by the woodsy smell of his cologne clinging to it, as I re-played his smile in my mind.

seven

I STUMBLED INTO THE KITCHEN, my eyes barely opened and my hair was a mess from tossing in the night. Parker was already there, sitting at the kitchen island with a bowl of cereal in front of him, chewing obnoxiously.

"Morning," he said without looking up, his spoon diving in for another scoop. "You're up early."

"Couldn't sleep well," I admitted, rubbing the sleep from my eyes.

He finally glanced up, his eyes narrowing as they landed on the oversized sweatshirt I had on. "You still have on Reese's hoodie?"

I wrapped my arms around myself, suddenly conscious of the soft fabric that still had his scent clinging to it. "Yeah, it got chilly last night, and he offered it to me... It's comfy."

Parker's eyebrow quirked up, with a questionable look on his face. But before he could voice his thoughts, I reached for a mug, hoping to distract him from questioning me further about it.

"Want some coffee?" I asked, forcing a small smile as I started to refill the water in the coffee machine.

"Sure," his gaze lingered on the sweatshirt as if signaling that I should probably take it off. "I'm guessing you didn't see the argument between Boston and Reese last night?"

I paused, the mug I was holding nearly slipping from my grasp. "Argument? No, what happened?"

He sat his bowl down on the counter. "It happened in the hallway at the party. They started shoving each other, and I thought they were going to throw down right there."

"Seriously?" I leaned back against the counter, surprised. Boston wasn't one to start fights, but I knew he wouldn't back down either. I wondered when this could have happened—probably at some point when Willow was introducing me to people around the party.

"Reese has always had a smart mouth and a temper," Parker's eyes met mine, with a glint of concern. "It looked like maybe they bumped into each other, which started it. Then, he told Boston not to forget whose team he was on. That it was his."

"His team?" Who did he think he was? The Blue Devils belonged to no one. Boston was just as much a part of that team as Reese was.

"Yep," Parker said under his breath. "He threatened to have Boston thrown off the team if he didn't watch himself. I don't get why he's always had something against him."

"Me either. Why does Reese think he owns the team?"

"He pretty much does," he shrugged. "That's why he's so cocky."

"Because of his dad?" I asked.

"Yeah, his dad pays for everything. Without his donations, I don't know if there would be a team. Probably why he acts untouchable."

"Wow..." I searched for the right words, feeling the heat from the mug radiate into my palms. "That's messed up. I had no idea that happened."

"You know how Bayside is—filled with privilege and power." Parker reached for his mug, blowing on the surface before taking a cautious sip. "Hope they can pull their shit together before our first game next week."

I nodded nervously, now worried about how the game was going to go.

"Speaking of," he said, crumpling a napkin in his hand with a simple motion, "I'll wake up Boston while you get dressed. We gotta get to the field."

I paused mid-sip as I turned to face him, my movements punctuated by a sense of sudden intrusion into my planned lazy morning. "Why do I have to go?"

"Because," Parker continued, clearly annoyed he had to explain further, "We have to go grocery shopping after we get our uniforms." He opened the empty fridge and pointed inside.

I let out an exaggerated huff, dropping my cup in the sink. "Fine."

I quickly changed into an outfit that Parker would deem more appropriate and tagged along.

"Chandler, come on! Coach said he'd have the uniforms ready by now," Parker called back to me, frustrated that I wasn't keeping up with him and Boston.

"Right behind you!" I hoisted the strap of my bag higher onto my shoulder and picked up my pace.

Parker and Boston disappeared into the clubhouse, leaving me standing alone outside the building. I noticed a group of people playing a casual game of softball. They were all having a good time, laughing and teasing each other. My eyes immediately landed on Reese, who was pitching, of course—and looking as gorgeous as ever despite the scorching heat.

"Chandler!" Willow spotted me and jogged over. "Come be on my team! We need one more player to bat."

"Willow, I don't know—" I began, hesitating as I looked over my shoulder for Parker or Boston.

"Come on, it'll be fun!" Her bubbly personality was hard to resist. "Don't make me beg."

"Alright, fine," I conceded with a laugh, dropping my bag to the ground as I followed behind her.

"Besides," she whispered as I followed her, "you get to bat

against Reese. Maybe knock that cocky smile off his face when you hit a home run."

"One can only dream," I laughed, eyeing Reese's confident stance on the mound. His eyes flicked toward us briefly, acknowledging my approach with a slight nod.

"Chandler's up!" Willow announced to the field, and a few heads turned—some with curiosity, others with a smile that the game was back in action.

"Let's see what you've got, little Hartford," Reese taunted.

With a deep breath, I squared up to the plate, determined to focus, to hit it as hard as I could back at Reese, to show him that I had much more in me than just Parker's little sister.

I took my stance at home plate, and he locked eyes with me before he lifted his shirt to wipe the sweat from his face, revealing a flash of those unfairly sculpted and perfectly toned abs.

"Bring it in close, boys!" he yelled out to the outfielders with an impish smirk as he made a gesture with his hand. I narrowed my eyes and tightened my grip on the bat, angry that he would underestimate me.

"Jerk," I whispered under my breath, as I leaned in closer to the plate.

"Did you say something?" he raised his chin.

"Just throw the ball," I snapped back.

"You asked for it," he drawled before winding up.

Reese's smirk grew as he started his windup, but I knew something he didn't—I wasn't some amateur. He had no idea how many days I spent practicing and playing in the backyard with Parker and Boston.

His pitch came hurtling towards me, and I was ready. The ball rocketed off the bat, aimed straight at Reese's ego.

"Nice hit!" a voice from behind me cheered, and I knew without looking it was Willow. It bolstered my confidence as I watched the ball do exactly what I'd intended—served as a fuck off to Reese.

It just missed his head as he ducked—a flash of surprise in his smug eyes. The line drive shot past him, soaring far beyond what the outfielders had anticipated. They scrambled back, their shoes kicking up dirt and grass, but the ball was beyond their reach, slicing through the field.

I shot a wink at Reese and didn't wait to see where it landed. Then, with a nonchalant flick of the wrist, I tossed the bat aside and walked off the field. My heart pounded—not just for the hit, but for the obvious message sent. I could still feel Reese's gaze on me as I walked away, burning with something that might have been respect—or maybe the sting of being shown up around his friends.

Boston smiled as he watched by the clubhouse. He leaned against the brick wall, his arms crossed. "Too bad you just missed him."

"Missed?" I echoed, reaching for my bag and slinging it over my shoulder. "I didn't miss. Just wanted to give him a warning this time." I smiled and shrugged innocently.

"Warning, huh?" Parker laughed, bumping fists with me. "Well, consider the message received. Loud and clear."

"I think that's game, my friends!" Parker yelled out, the excitement lacing his words enough to draw snickers from a few of their teammates.

There was no stopping the smile that spread across my face with satisfaction as I left the field behind me.

A week later, the sun beat down on the back of my neck as I sat in the bleachers—the metal benches were scorching beneath me. My heart pounded with excitement and nerves as I watched the players warming up on the field below.

Boston shot a wink at me before catching the ball and tossing it back to Parker. They were both dressed in their new uniforms, the bright white pants and bold blue jerseys were gleaming.

Willow plopped down on the bench beside me with two cold sodas in hand. "Here," she sighed, passing me one. "It's so hot out here. I'm practically melting."

"Thanks." I pressed the icy can to my cheek, relishing the coolness.

"I hope they do well today," she shielded her eyes from the sun as she watched the team practice. "Dad's nervous, I can tell."

"Your dad really knows how to inspire them," I responded, watching the coach get the players pumped up for the game.

"Yep, he's been coaching for as long as I can remember," Willow added. "I've loved every minute of watching him. You know, I want to be just like him one day."

"Coaching?" I asked, surprised but intrigued.

"Absolutely!" Willow bubbled with excitement. "Whether it's softball or even breaking into the baseball world, I want to make a difference, just like he does. It's not just about teaching the game, it's about building confidence, and creating a team that's more like a family."

I laughed softly, admiring her ambition. "I can totally see you doing that, Willow. And shaking things up while you're at it."

"For sure." Willow's smile was full of promise. "Just wait and see. I'm going to coach a team to victory one day."

I cracked open my soda. "Well, Boston was talking nonstop about this game. And I know Parker wants to impress all the girls here today, too," I said with a laugh.

Willow rolled her eyes good-naturedly.

The announcer's voice suddenly boomed over the loudspeaker, jolting me from my thoughts. "Alright folks, it's time for the first pitch…"

Reese appeared from out of the dugout and walked to the mound, confident in every step.

Around me, girls whispered and giggled.

"There's Reese, he's so hot."

"I know, right? Those eyes…" another sighed dreamily.

I rolled my eyes and looked away. Of course, they were drooling over him. As he went into his motion on the mound, his muscles flexed, and the green of his eyes flashed brightly beneath his cap.

A tiny part of me understood their awe. With his bad-boy reputation, dangerous charm, and wealthy family, Willow said that Reese had always drawn attention from all the girls in town. I wondered if there was more to him underneath the surface.

A few rows up, Blair leapt to her feet, clapping and cheering as Reese threw his first pitch. "Let's go, Reese!" she shouted. "You got this, babe!"

I exhaled, sinking lower in my seat. Blair, the perfect, beautiful girlfriend was back to claim her territory. She was wearing a shirt with the number two on it, Reese's number.

As the game ended, the crowd erupted into cheers as number twenty-nine, Boston, slid into home plate, sealing the victory for the team. Parker jumped up from the dugout, pumping his fist in the air. I couldn't help but grin from ear to ear, my heart swelled with pride for them.

They all played so well today. Parker did great behind the plate and Boston had three outs at shortstop plus the game-winning run. He was glowing as he high-fived his teammates, flashing that signature crooked smile that made all the girls swoon. And Reese, he had pitched a hell of a game. Sure, he was arrogant, but there was no denying his talent.

As the team gathered around home plate, I saw Reese approach Parker with his hand held out for a fist bump. Parker returned it enthusiastically and said something that made Reese laugh. Before I knew it, Boston had joined them, and the three of them were celebrating their victory. I never thought I'd see the day when Reese and Boston were on the same team, let alone winning together. I guess I had underestimated their sportsmanship. Maybe underneath the rivalry, they respected each other as athletes.

eight

WILLOW and I waited for Parker and Boston in the bleachers after the rest of the crowd emptied, ready to celebrate. We noticed Boston first as he jogged over. His wavy hair was tousled and damp with sweat, and his jersey was covered in dirt. Before I could stand, he swept me up into a fierce hug, practically lifting me into the air.

"You did it!" I cheered, hugging him back tightly.

He set me down, grinning from ear to ear. "Did you see that last inning? We smashed it!"

Parker ran over, slinging an arm around Boston's shoulders. "All thanks to this guy's batting skills. MVP for sure!"

Boston waved him off, though his cheeks flushed pink at the praise. Behind them, the rest of the team cheered loudly, already stripping off their jerseys and making a beeline for the lake just beyond the field, ready to celebrate their victory.

Boston watched them go, then turned back to me, his smile softening.

"C'mon," he said, holding out his hand. "Let's join the party."

I laced my fingers through his, while we raced to catch up with the others. Parker looked over at Willow. "Keep up, babe," he shouted, breaking into a run and pulling her along toward the shimmering lake. Willow squealed but kept pace with him, her feet were pounding against the sandy shore. She threw her purse and phone on the nearest picnic table and I did the same. As they reached the water's edge, Parker scooped Willow up into his arms, eliciting another delighted shriek from her.

"Don't you dare throw me in!" Willow demanded, laughing as she clung to his shoulders.

Parker waded into the cool water up to his knees. "What, you don't trust me?" He grinned mischievously.

Willow narrowed her eyes at him. "Parker Hartford, if you throw me in fully clothed, I'll…"

Her threat was cut off as Parker tossed her into the air. She flailed for a moment before she hit the water with a tremendous splash. Parker burst into laughter as Willow came up sputtering, her sopping wet hair covering her face.

"You are so freaking dead!" Willow shouted, but she was laughing too as she sloshed over to Parker and shoved him. He toppled backwards into the water. When he emerged, they were both cracking up.

One by one, the team leapt and dove into the lake.

I took small steps in, savoring the moment. The cool water felt amazing after being out in the hot sun all day. I found my way to Willow. Her blonde curls were already frizzing in the humidity.

"What a game," she sighed contently.

"Yeah," I smiled. "There's a lot of talent on the team."

"Speaking of the game… Parker!" Willow began, her voice sounded serious. "You know, if you had positioned your feet just a smidge differently, you could've snagged those two balls in the fifth."

Parker turned to face her, the corners of his mouth twitching upward despite the critique. "Yeah?" he asked, genuinely curious. "You'll have to show me what you mean."

"I would have before you threw me in the lake," she rolled her eyes.

"Whatever you say, Coach," he teased, bumping her shoulder lightly with his own.

"Has a pretty great ring to it, don't you think?" Willow grinned, a spark of ambition lighting up her eyes.

"I'd take orders from you over your dad any day." Parker smiled back.

We floated lazily, watching the rowdy team enjoy their victory swim. Parker and Boston were dunking each other playfully, their boyish laughter echoing across the lake.

My heart swelled with happiness. Not all games end this way, but today was one of those perfect moments you wanted to bottle up and save forever. That moment ended quickly once I noticed that something was going on with Boston.

"I'll be right back," Boston shouted before he walked out of the lake. Water dripped down his tanned shoulders as he jogged over to his belongings. I watched him pull his phone out, and his eyes narrowed when he saw who it was.

"Really, Mom?" he growled into the phone. His jaw clenched, fingers drumming against his thigh. He listened for a moment, then sighed heavily. "You always say you have to work. I really wanted you at my first game. I don't get why you can't ever make one." He sighed before continuing. "Well, I'm telling you now that I want you at the big game against our cross-town rivals. Coach said some of the pro scouts will be there, and you should be too. It gives you plenty of time to request off."

Ending the call, he shoved the phone into his bag. I saw his chest rise and fall as he took a deep breath, trying to calm himself. Then he put a shirt on before he walked closer to us, just before the edge of the water.

"I'm gonna go for a walk," he called out, running a hand through his damp curls.

Parker treaded closer, concern etching his features. "You good, bro?"

Boston's shoulders lifted in a shrug that seemed too heavy.

"Yeah, all good. Just need to clear my head," his voice carried a forced lightness. "I'll be back in a bit."

As he turned away, I caught the shadow that passed over his face, the same one that appeared every time he had ended a call with his mom.

"Sure thing. Let me know if you need some company," Parker responded, but his gaze lingered on Boston's retreating back, unsure if Boston was really okay.

"She has never missed a single college game, you know? I don't get why she can't ever make it to Bayside. Do you think something happened to her here when she was younger?" I asked, my words were a mix of frustration and empathy.

"I don't know. I don't get it either," Parker said solemnly.

"Poor kid." Willow shook her head in sympathy.

"I'm gonna go dry off and lay out for a bit," I yelled to Parker and Willow as I headed out of the lake. They waved absently before quickly returning to their playful splashing and laughter.

I made my way toward the edge of the water, looking in Boston's direction, but he was already out of sight, so I decided to take a seat on the dock nearby. As I approached, I saw someone's long legs hanging over the side. It was Reese. I didn't realize that he had also walked away from the group.

"Shit," I whispered under my breath. He chose that moment to glance up, his eyes meeting mine. There was no mistaking it—he had seen me. His eyes squinted in the sunlight. "Hartford," he said smoothly, a hint of a smile playing on his lips. "To what do I owe the pleasure? Planning on trying to kill me again?"

I couldn't turn back now, not without it being more awkward than simply facing him. With a resigned sigh, I resumed my approach, each step feeling heavier than the last.

"Only if you tempt me... and do you call every girl by their last name, Carrington?" I asked, taking another small step closer to him.

"Only the pretty ones," he replied with a roguish wink. His gaze drifted down, lingering on my lips for a while before meeting my eyes again.

The intensity of his eyes made my heart pick up speed. Get it together, Chandler. I held his stare, refusing to be the first to look away. I wasn't convinced by his smooth words.

"Whatever. I guess you pitched a good game," I forced out.

"You should expect nothing less from me. I aim to please," he winked.

I pushed a strand of hair behind my ear. "I'm sure... Anyway, I'll leave you alone. I didn't realize anyone was sitting here."

"All good," he said with a crooked grin. I smiled back before turning and walking away.

"Hey, wait up a sec," Reese called after me from the dock.

I turned slowly back to look at him, raising an eyebrow.

He hesitated, almost shyly. "Do you wanna see something? My favorite spot is right up this hill." He pointed a finger at a nearby area on his right.

"What kind of spot?" I said, curiosity getting the better of me. I couldn't put my finger on what was drawing me to him. All I knew was that being around Reese gave me a thrill I'd never felt before.

"You have to see it for yourself," he said with a grin. "But I think you'll dig it. That is, if you're up for a little adventure?" He raised an eyebrow in challenge.

How could I say no when he was looking at me like that? Although I was unsure about him, I felt a calmness and a comfortability with him that I couldn't explain. I pretended to consider it before smiling back and throwing caution to the wind. "Lead the way."

nine

WE WALKED IN SILENCE, eventually coming up to a beautiful two-story cottage I'd never seen before.

"Where are we?" I asked, taking in the beauty of the landscaping on the property.

"My uncle's place," Reese explained. "He's out of town a lot."

He led me around the side of the cottage, where I saw the most stunning backyard with an in-ground pool. The water was crystal blue and shimmering in the sunlight. My eyes widened.

"This is gorgeous!"

Reese smiled, pleased by my reaction. "Wait until you see the view of the lake from the pool."

I followed him toward the pool deck, taking in my surroundings. Being here with Reese felt special, like he could be here with anyone, but for some odd reason, he wanted to be here with me.

"C'mon, let's jump in," Reese said eagerly, pulling his shirt over his head.

My eyes immediately gravitated to his sculpted body, the defined muscles rippled with every breath he took. I blushed and looked away. "Get a grip, Chandler!" I scolded myself.

"What's the matter, Hartford? You chicken?"

I rolled my eyes, attempting to conceal my thoughts. "You wish."

He took a running start, cannonballing into the pool. I laughed and jumped in after him, and we came up gasping.

"Not bad, but your cannonball needs a little work," Reese said, pushing his wet hair back.

We joked back and forth, our banter flowed easily. Reese's laugh was cute and melodic, and I didn't hate hearing it. Then, the playful mood shifted, and our eyes locked. A blush rose to my cheeks as we took a moment to catch our breath. There was an intensity in his emerald eyes that made me nervous.

"So..." I said, looking down at my hands in the water to try to calm my nerves. "This view is amazing. It feels like we're swimming right on top of the lake. Do you come here a lot?"

Lame small talk, but I couldn't think straight with him looking at me like that.

"Sometimes," he said. "When I want to get away from everything. It's peaceful here."

I paused, silently wondering what kind of things he wanted to escape from. He seemed like the type of person who could have anything he wanted—whenever he wanted.

"I was hoping I'd get to talk to you again after the party." Reese's voice broke through the brief moment of silence.

His interest took me by surprise. I peered at him, searching his eyes for any hint of his usual cockiness, but found none. "What did you want to talk about?" I asked cautiously.

"More about you." His answer was simple, yet it piqued my interest. He leaned back against the pool edge, arms stretched out along the tiled border, casual yet somehow commanding. "I'm intrigued by you," he said, softly. "I like that you're not caught up in the drama of Bayside, and your line drives are pretty impressive."

"Is that so?" I teased, keeping my tone light. "And here I thought you enjoyed all the attention and being in the center of the drama."

"Maybe—sometimes it's entertaining," he conceded with a sly

grin. "But there's something refreshing about someone who isn't a part of it. Like you."

"Be careful, Carrington. Someone might think you were actually trying to be kind," I joked, splashing water in his direction playfully.

Reese's eyes glinted with mischief as he pushed off from the pool's edge to float closer. "Don't tell anyone," he said, flashing a smile. "I wouldn't want anyone to think there's anything kind about me."

"Your secret's safe with me," I joked, trying to play it cool as my heart raced because the space between us was shrinking.

The embarrassing truth was that no matter how cool I tried to play it around him, he made it impossible for me to ignore his appeal. His self-assurance, charm, toned body—that was now just a few inches away.

"So..." he said, his curiosity evident. "What's the deal with you and Riley?"

"Huh? Boston? What do you mean?" I asked, caught off guard.

Reese raised an eyebrow. "Come on, I see the way he looks at you. He's totally into you."

My cheeks flushed. "No way, he'd never look at me like that. He's Parker's best friend, and we've just known each other forever—practically since diapers."

"There's more to it than that, I can tell," Reese said genuinely before he asked, "You aren't hoping he'll ask you to the Bayside Ball?"

"No," I answered. "I honestly don't think it sounds that fun."

"You don't hear that often around here," he smirked—not his usual, confident smirk, but it seemed more genuine, almost fascinated.

"Well, I'm not from Bayside," I reminded him.

"Speaking of Boston.." I began, hesitantly. He raised an eyebrow in that infuriatingly arrogant way of his.

"What about him?" Reese's jaw tightened almost immediately. His tone was casual, but his body was tense.

"I know you two have been competitive over the years. And don't say it has been in a friendly, joking way—something feels more serious than that." I watched Reese's face carefully as I spoke. "You are teammates now and you need to work together."

Reese was silent for a moment, looking away in the distance. When he finally spoke, his voice was low. "It's just normal guy stuff. It's nothing you need to worry about."

I moved even closer, forcing him to make eye contact with me. "You seriously need to let it go."

Reese held my gaze for a long moment before he replied. "Fine, I'll work on it." He forced a small smile. "But no promises."

I sighed, knowing this was the best I was going to get from him for now. The tension between Reese and Boston worried me, but at least I had opened the dialogue a bit more. For now, that would have to be enough.

"And you asked me about Boston, but don't you have a girl-friend?" I asked, deflecting. "You two seem like a cute couple."

"Nah, it's not like that." He shook his head. "We're not together anymore. Me and Blair just hook up sometimes when it's convenient for her. She's kinda possessive over me, but she's always been that way—I guess it's more of a friends-with-benefits thing."

"Well, Boston and I don't have any benefits," I said firmly.

Reese smiled, a dimple flashing in his cheek. "Good to know, but benefits can be the best part."

I raised an eyebrow. "I'm sure you'd think that," I retorted, a playful edge to my tone.

Reese gave a subtle smile, his smoldering eyes locking onto mine with an intensity that was both disarming and enticing. He leaned in closer, his tone smooth as silk and just as dangerous. "I bet you'd like benefits with me," he whispered, the words hanging between us like a tantalizing promise.

His gaze never wavered from mine, daring me to react. "Look, I'll give you two options," he continued, his voice low and tempting. "Get out of the pool like I think you'll probably do." he paused, a flicker of challenge. "Or stay... and let me show you."

My heart hammered in my chest, but I found myself anchored to the spot. There was no room for words, only the anticipation buzzing between us. I remained still, unblinking, as if challenging his threat.

Then, with a fluidity that matched the ripples surrounding us, Reese closed the little distance left. His hands slid smoothly around my waist. I sucked in a breath, dizzy from his woodsy cologne and the intoxicating nearness of him.

Reese tilted my chin up. His eyes searched mine, apparently finding consent there, then he slowly lowered his mouth on mine.

My eyelids fluttered shut. The kiss started slow and tender, as if he was testing the waters, unsure if I'd stop him. His lips were soft and tentative, then more intense. His tongue felt warm as he slipped it into my mouth, as though it were casually flirting with mine. I could almost taste the cocky smirk on his face, and even worse—I liked it. I placed my arms over his broad shoulders, melting into his embrace-—feeling his strong chest against mine. I couldn't get enough of him.

I thought I knew what a kiss was supposed to be, but Reese taught me otherwise. His mouth moved against mine with an expertise that should have been alarming for how fast it made my heart race. But instead, it felt like paradise. His hands were strong, and he knew exactly where to place them, cradling my face as his thumb brushed my cheek in a tenderness that didn't echo his bad-boy reputation.

When we finally broke apart, my body felt like it was drifting away. I opened my eyes slowly, unprepared for the rush of sensations that left me feeling untethered, as if gravity had loosened its grip just for me—to allow me the kindness of floating on this cloud just a while longer.

"Fuck, I knew you were into me," he drew in a long breath, the corners of his mouth lifting into an arrogant, yet endearing smile.

"Shut up," I splashed him playfully, and I couldn't help but smile. Kissing him was different from any kiss I'd had before. It wasn't like those clumsy, fleeting encounters during spin the bottle in Kithma

Kennedy's basement. I had a few drunken flings this past year that never ended up escalating to sex. But, none of those encounters had made me feel the way he just did.

No, this kiss... it was as if every nerve ending came alive, sparking a sensation that was all-consuming and entirely new.

We both rested our backs near the edge of the pool, taking a moment to relax. "We should probably get back to the others," Reese said, his gaze flickering to me. "Before they send out a search party."

I snickered. "You're right." I couldn't help but see the mental image of Willow organizing our friends into some search party with maps and flashlights in hand. The confidence in her navigation skills would be endearing, but a bit misplaced.

"By the way, some friends are coming over tomorrow night. Just another get-together at my place. You should stop by if you're free."

I smiled at him softly. "I'll think about it."

We stood up and Reese took my hand, intertwining our fingers. I couldn't help but notice the contrast between his strong, calloused hand and my delicate one. The warmth of his touch made me feel safe and connected to him in that moment.

"Come on, I'll lead the way," he said with a roguish grin, holding my hand down a narrow path through the trees and down the hill.

We crept back towards the water, trying not to attract any attention. The sounds of the others laughing and talking echoed across the still lake. I tiptoed back into the cool water, the mud squishing between my toes.

Willow floated on her back just a few feet away, her blonde hair fanning out around her, oblivious to my temporary disappearance as Parker was talking her ear off. Boston had returned and was talking to another player nearby. Taking a deep breath, I leaned back and let the water hold me up too, staring at the clouds drifting slowly above us. For now, I could pretend I hadn't just been fraternizing with the enemy. I could pretend everything was normal. But the gnawing guilt remained, an undercurrent threatening to take me down at any moment.

I peeked over at Reese, talking to a group of players who were drying off like he didn't have a care in the world. How could he be so calm when my heart was pounding out of my chest? All I could do now was float here, acting natural, while my mind spun in endless circles, trying to process it all.

On the ride home, I couldn't help but notice a strange expression on Boston's face as he focused on the road.

"So... what's going on with you and Reese?" he asked, a hardness to his tone.

I glanced over at him in surprise. "What do you mean?"

"I saw you guys talking earlier," Boston said, his jaw tight.

My cheeks flushed. I stared down at my hands. "There's nothing going on," I mumbled. I honestly wasn't sure what was going on or what was even happening.

Boston was silent for a moment, then he swallowed hard, looking away. "Just be careful, okay? Reese isn't as charming as he seems."

"Woah," Parker called out from the back seat of the car, popping his head up between Boston and me. "Something between Chandler and Reese Carrington? Ha! That would never happen."

I rolled my eyes, trying to ignore the annoyance that bubbled up inside of me. I glanced at Boston, who seemed equally unimpressed with Parker's comment.

"Really, Parker? How would you know?" I sighed, shaking my head.

"Come on, it's Reese Carrington. He is constantly surrounded by hot girls and you're like the opposite of a hot girl..." Parker teased. "Now, on to more realistic topics... The real question is, how into me is Willow? I think I spotted her checking out my abs."

Willow being into Parker? Boston and I couldn't help but laugh. It was hard to stay annoyed when Parker was being ridiculous. The laughter felt like a release, as if some of the tension that had been building between us had momentarily dissipated.

"I can't stand you," I said, wiping away a tear that had escaped during our laughter. "You got us, Parker. I'll admit, Willow's annoyance with you seems to be subsiding just a bit. I think I saw her laugh at one of your stupid jokes."

"Ha! I knew it!" Parker said triumphantly, sinking back into the back seat with a satisfied grin.

"Good for you, buddy," Boston chimed in, giving Parker a playful wink. "Just don't let it go to your head."

"Of course not," Parker responded, emphasizing innocence. "I'm just happy to finally have someone who appreciates my amazing sense of humor."

"Amazing might be a bit of a stretch," I teased, smirking at him in the rearview mirror.

ten

THE NEXT DAY, I sat on the edge of Willow's bed, my legs folded under me. Her room smelled like lavender and old books. I knew that I needed to talk to someone about Reese and I still wasn't having much luck at getting a hold of Kristina. "So..." I said, while I picked at a loose thread on her comforter. "Reese kissed me yesterday."

Willow's eyes went wide. She leaned forward, gripping my hands. "He did what? Oh, my god! I can't believe it!" Her smile faded. "Wait. When? What about Blair?"

I sighed, flopping back on the bed. "We snuck away for a little while when we were at the lake and I don't know about Blair," I admitted. "He said that they weren't together, and I was caught up in the moment, but I probably shouldn't have trusted he was telling me the truth. Maybe I need to talk to Blair? And make sure?"

Willow nodded sympathetically. "Well, how do you feel about him? Do you like him?"

I stared up at the ceiling. Did I like Reese? His confidence, his bright green eyes, the feeling of his lips on mine...

"Yeah," I sighed. "Unfortunately, I think I do."

Willow squealed and threw her hands in the air. "Oh, this is so exciting! So what's going to happen next?"

I sat up again. "Well, he said he's having some friends over tonight."

"Eek!" Willow bounced a little on the bed. "Well, then we're going!"

I bit my lip. "I just don't know if it's a good idea. My family would probably flip if they knew. I feel like I shouldn't keep putting myself in these situations when I know it can't go anywhere."

Willow waved her hand. "It'll be fine! Don't worry so much." She grinned. "You never know where it could lead. And you don't have to decide anything tonight. Just enjoy yourself."

I still felt unsure, but I hoped she was right. My mind drifted back to the kiss, thinking about Reese's soft lips against mine. The memory brought back a flood of feelings.

I nodded, feeling uneasy. "I hope so. I just can't stop thinking about that kiss. What did it mean, you know? Does he actually like me?"

Willow squeezed my arm reassuringly. "Of course he does! Why else would he kiss you?"

"I honestly don't know." I frowned. "Maybe it didn't mean anything. Maybe he does this with all the girls."

"No way." Willow shook her head firmly. "I've seen girls throw themselves at him before, and he doesn't entertain very many. He could have anyone he wanted, and he kissed you. That boy has to be into you."

I felt a glimmer of hope. "You really think so?"

"Absolutely." Willow smiled. "I wouldn't worry about it. This is what summer is about. Maybe it will go somewhere, maybe it won't. But I do know one thing, you and I are going to have fun along the way, girlfriend!"

I took a deep breath. Willow somehow knew how to make me feel better. "You're right. I'm overthinking this."

"That's my girl," Willow sprang up and headed for her closet.

"Now, what are you going to wear? We need to make sure you look hot."

I laughed as she began rifling through her clothes. No matter what happened, at least I'd have Willow by my side. I knew she'd always be in my corner.

A couple of hours later, Willow and I stepped into Reese's house. This party was even bigger than his last. I thought this would be a small get-together, but this was definitely a full-blown party. I scanned the crowded foyer, searching for those familiar green eyes, but only found unfamiliar faces flushed with alcohol.

"Are his parents ever around?" I said loudly in Willow's ear.

"I think his family travels in the summer. He stays here for baseball. But I'm going to go get us a drink," Willow yelled over the music.

I continued to make my way through the house and was just about to give up my search for Reese when I spotted him through the open doorway of the kitchen—or rather, a glimpse of his dark hair with a look of annoyance in his eyes. He was with Blair, engaged in what appeared to be an intense conversation.

Curiosity piqued as I quietly approached the doorway and positioned myself just around the corner, out of their sight, but close enough to see their heated exchange out of the corner of my eye.

"We always fall back into the same pattern," I heard him say, frustration evident in his voice. "We both want something more, so maybe it's time we actually cut it off completely and do something different."

"What about the Bayside Ball?" She persisted, her manicured hands clenched at her sides.

He exhaled sharply, his eyes not meeting hers. "Blair," he said, his voice low and steady, "the last time I took you, you spent the whole night on your phone. Now you don't have to worry about it."

Her expression shifted, Blair looked as if she'd been slapped. "Are you serious right now?" She scoffed, clearly offended by his statement. "I could have anyone I want. I could go to the Bayside Ball with anyone I want. You'd regret it if you really pushed me away this time."

I could hear the ice clinking against the glass as Reese took a sip of his drink before responding. "It's not about that... we're stuck in this cycle that isn't making either of us happy. We hook up or attend whatever dumb work event our dads force us to go to, and we hardly even talk some days. Don't you want a real relationship with someone? We need to stop doing the same shit over and over."

It struck me then that beneath Reese's carefree attitude, there was a hidden depth to him—he wanted something more substantial. Compassion resonated within me, as I could hear the sadness in his voice. As their argument continued, I realized this was a side of Reese that he didn't show very often. It was a side that drew me in even more.

Blair slammed her drink down on the counter and sounded even more angry now. "Fine. But don't come running back to me again when you realize the mistake you've made."

"Just listen," Reese sighed, as if the weight of their history was heavy on his shoulders. "I'm not trying to hurt you. I want something better for both of us. You don't deserve some half-ass relationship."

I held my breath while I waited for her response, but she remained silent. A tense moment passed before I heard the sound of footsteps approaching toward the doorway. Panicking, I quickly moved further into the shadows, hoping they hadn't noticed my presence. As she stormed past, her stiletto heels were clicking angrily against the hardwood floor.

I knew it wasn't the right time, but I couldn't help wondering what this might mean for Reese and me. This boy who held everyone at arm's length was searching for something deeper. The thought of exploring that depth alongside him—and what that would be like was something I couldn't wrap my head around.

Wanting to get as far away as I could from what had just happened, I walked around until I found Willow again in the crowd.

She smiled warmly at me, the kind of bright smile that could put anyone at ease.

"There you are! Did you find Reese?" she asked, handing me a drink and inching closer so she could hear me over the music.

"No, but it's okay, he's here somewhere—I'll bump into him at some point," I responded, taking a sip of the drink, trying not to think about Reese and Blair's argument that I shouldn't have been listening to.

"Let's dance!" Willow shouted, pulling me into the center of the group. As we danced and sang along to the lyrics, I couldn't help but begin to let loose, allowing any worry I had from earlier to melt away. I was lost in the moment of being surrounded by friends. Our voices and laughter blended together as one.

But then, as I twirled around, my eyes locked with Reese's across the room. He was leaning against the wall with a group of his friends nearby, his intense gaze never leaving me. There was an extremely hot smirk on his lips, making me suddenly feel the heat under his stare. My heart raced, and I froze--suddenly feeling like I was under a spotlight.

"Chandler, I don't hear you singing!" Willow's voice pulled me back to reality.

I continued to sing along with her, trying to shake off the feeling of knowing he was watching. Still, I couldn't help but continue to glance at him from time to time, wondering what thoughts were running through his mind as he watched me. Was it all in my mind, or was that smoldering look in his eyes filled with desire?

THE POUNDING bass of the music vibrated through my chest. Willow and I had been dancing for a while now, and my eyes darted to Reese every so often. I couldn't help but think about what had transpired between him and Blair and whether it had anything to do with me.

"I have no idea where I put my drink. My song came on and I got too excited... I think I threw it somewhere." Willow snickered, spinning me around in time with the beat. As I turned, I saw that Reese's gaze found mine once again. This time, however, he was making his way through the crowd and was headed in my direction. I swallowed, anticipation and anxiety began to flutter within me.

"Hey," Reese said smoothly as he reached me, his hand rested gently on my arm. "Can I talk to you for a second?"

"Uh, sure," I stammered, feeling the eyes of everyone around us as he led me away. The music seemed to fade into the background as we moved further away from everyone else.

"Is everything okay?" I asked, trying to ignore the butterflies in my stomach.

"Everything's fine," he assured me, with a gentle smile. Then, he leaned in so close that his lips brushed against my ear as he whispered, "You look so damn good tonight. I can't take my eyes off you."

My breath was caught in my throat at his words, warmth flooding my cheeks. It was as if everyone around us had faded away, leaving only the two of us and the undeniable chemistry that sparked between us.

"Reese, I—" I started, unsure of what to say or how to react.

"I just couldn't help myself. I had to pull you away," he said with a slight smirk, clearly enjoying the effect he had on me. "I wanna kiss you again."

"We shouldn't," I breathed out, trying to keep my composure. His words had left me reeling, but at the same time, I knew what had just happened with him and Blair. I knew she was here somewhere and it wouldn't be right.

I wanted to lean into him, to let him wrap his arms around me and give in to the desire that burned between us. But I couldn't. Not after hearing the argument he'd just had. It wasn't fair to Blair—who could walk by any moment, heartbroken or upset.

He pulled back slightly, confusion flickered in his eyes. "Why not?"

My mind raced, searching for a way to explain without revealing that I'd overheard his argument. "Because I know Blair's here, Reese. I can't come between whatever the two of you have going on. And most of the team is here too—if anything gets back to Parker, he'd be so pissed."

"Is that all you're worried about?" He chuckled softly, his eyes never leaving mine. "Parker doesn't own you. You can make your own choices. And I told you, Blair isn't my girlfriend."

"We just can't," I said softly, barely a whisper. "We shouldn't have even kissed before."

Feeling overwhelmed, I leaned against the wall as I let out the breath I was holding. Reese followed, all six feet plus of him leaned in even closer—casting a shadow over me. He rested one arm above my head on the wall, his warm breath brushed across the side of my face.

"Okay," he murmured, before slightly shifting his head to the side. "So you're telling me you don't want me to kiss you here?" His fingers lightly grazed my neck, tracing a path that sent an ache through my whole body. I bit my lip, struggling to keep my breathing under control. The desire coursing through me was undeniable, but I knew I couldn't give in.

"No, I don't," I whispered, my voice shaking with the effort of keeping him at bay.

"Are you sure?" His voice was low and seductive. "You have no idea how much I want you right now." His fingers trace a tantalizing path from my neck to my ear. With a gentle push, he brushed my hair back, exposing the sensitive skin beneath. "It seems like your body is saying something else."

My body was betraying me. That's what it was doing. "I'm sure," I managed to choke out, trying to keep my voice steady despite the turmoil inside me. My thoughts raced with conflicting emotions—I desperately wanted to kiss and touch him, but I knew I couldn't surrender to temptation.

Reese's voice was a low hum that vibrated through me, his breath still against my ear. "If you asked me nicely, I'd fuck you right here against this wall."

I felt every muscle in my body stiffen at his words. The reckless edge in his tone, laced with a challenge, made my heart feel like it was going to explode, and I swallowed hard, trying to regain some semblance of control over the situation.

"Good thing I'm not asking you," I said, somehow formulating the words.

"Alright," he breathed into my ear, sending a shudder through me. "When you change your mind, come find me." With a final lingering touch, he stepped back, leaving me leaning against the wall —my body was still tingling from his proximity.

As I watched him walk away, I fought the urge to call out to him, to give in to the passion that threatened to consume us both. Instead, I remained silent. My heart was feeling heavy with the weight of a decision I could only hope was the right one.

I took a seat in the nearest chair, needing a moment to catch my breath. Eventually, Willow's eager face pulled me out of the trance I was in. Her blue eyes were wide with urgency. "Chandler, you won't believe what I just heard!"

"Slow down. What happened?" I asked, feeling a knot form in the pit of my stomach.

"Okay, so Caroline told me that she walked into the bathroom, right? And there's Blair, mascara running down her cheeks, practically bawling her eyes out." Willow's features softened, betraying her sympathy. "She was telling her friends that Reese said he didn't want her to stay the night tonight... or stay over at all anymore."

"Reese said that?" I couldn't help but feel a strange mix of relief and concern for Blair at the same time.

"Yes, and I'm sure Caroline has told everyone by now that Blair is out of the picture." Willow leaned closer, lowering her voice. "This means there will probably be a competition of which girl is going to be his shoulder to cry on tonight. That shoulder should be yours."

"Are you serious? Why would they do that? Blair is the one who needs consoling."

"Chandler, come on," Willow rolled her eyes. "You know how girls around here are. It's Reese. He's hot, rich, a ticket to the Bayside ball, and all the things."

My heart raced at the thought of other girls comforting Reese, trying to get his attention. It wasn't fair—not to Blair, and not to Reese, who deserved better than to be pursued by someone trying to use him.

"Willow, I can't just go over there and compete to be some distraction or rebound," I said, hesitating. "I mean, it's not like I'm any different from the rest of them."

"Chandler," Willow placed her hands on my shoulders and

looked me straight in the eyes. "You are different. Now's your chance to be there for him. Trust me, you'll regret it if you don't."

I shook my head as I stared at the scene unfolding before me. "I can't, Willow. Not tonight. I don't want to step on anyone's toes." The last thing I wanted was to make things worse.

"Fine," Willow sighed, crossing her arms. "Let's just sit back and enjoy the show, then."

We sat in the distance, observing the group of girls that had gathered around Reese. They laughed too loud at his jokes and touched his arm more than necessary--it was painfully obvious what they were trying to do.

"Ugh, look at them," I exhaled. "You were right. They're practically throwing themselves at him."

"I wouldn't worry," Willow said, placing a comforting hand on my shoulder. "Reese is smarter than that. He'll see through their act."

"Maybe," I mumbled, unconvinced. My heart ached as I watched one girl lean in closer to Reese, whispering something into his ear that made him smile slightly. The jealousy simmering inside me threatened to boil over.

"Okay, that's enough," I declared, setting my drink down on the table. "I'm going to head home. I don't think I can keep watching this."

"Are you sure?" Willow said, standing up as she leaned in to give me a hug.

"I just want to go to bed and get some rest. I promise I'm fine."

As I walked away, I couldn't help but steal one last glance at Reese. He caught my eye and held my gaze for a brief moment, making my heart skip a beat. But then another girl draped her arm around him, pulling his attention back to her.

"FML," I whispered under my breath, feeling regret for not kissing Reese tonight when I had the chance.

twelve

THE SUN BEAMED in through my open window, which stirred me from sleep. I blinked against the harsh morning light and reached for my phone. Two new messages from a number I didn't recognize. My stomach dropped when I realized who it was.

> Unknown: Hey it's Reese. Willow finally caved and gave me your number after you left.

> Unknown: Why did you leave? I was kind of waiting for you to swoop in and save me from a strange girl who wouldn't leave me alone and kept calling me Ross.

I propped myself up on one elbow, rubbing my eyes and trying to make sense of what I was reading. Does that mean Reese didn't fall for one of those girls throwing themselves at him? I typed a reply, hesitating for a moment before hitting send.

> Did Willow really give you my number willingly, or did you have to pry it from her cold, dead hands? Is she alive, Ross?

I hear a soft chime from my phone as Reese responds almost instantly.

Reese: Very funny. Let's just say I can be very persuasive. But don't worry, I promised her I would be a gentleman.

Reese: Meet me at the marina near the field after practice today?

I'll think about it.

Reese: I'll take that as a yes.

I arrived at the marina. My palms were sweaty and my heart was pounding, unaware of what might be in store for me. As much as I tried to convince myself that this was just going to be a brief and casual encounter, I couldn't deny the fluttering in my stomach. That fluttering that had been happening a lot lately. I knew we kissed once, and it was incredible, but where could this even go?

I was well aware that I needed to keep my distance from Reese Carrington. Getting caught up in his whirlwind would probably bring chaos into my life, and I couldn't afford to let that happen. This wasn't a play—this was my actual life, and I was used to living in my safe, comfortable bubble. I knew I had to be cautious around him because of his reputation. Despite everything, it seemed as though the world shifted when we were together and the pull between us was too powerful to resist.

As soon as I spotted him, leaning against his speedboat with an air of nonchalance, I was struck by his presence. Reese's unreal eyes met mine, and a smile spread across his face, revealing those dimples. His golden deep tan seemed to glow beneath the sunlight.

"Hartford. Wasn't sure if you'd show. Hop on," He extended his hand towards me as he held the boat steady. The water lapped gently against the sides of the vessel as I hesitated for a moment before finally taking his offered hand. His grip was firm and reassuring, and I found myself reluctantly stepping onto the deck.

"Where are we going?" I asked, attempting to sound casual.

"Not far," he said, flashing me another one of his heart-stopping grins. "I figured we could just go for a ride and enjoy the view."

Reese started the boat's engine and looked effortlessly at ease, steering us into the open water with practiced skill. I couldn't help but admire the way he was so confident and calm in everything he did.

"Reese," I called out over the wind as we started to speed up, "why did you invite me here?" My voice wavered slightly, betraying my nerves.

He glanced back at me before he slowed the boat to a more relaxed pace. "Last night was... interesting," Reese replied cryptically, a mischievous grin tugging at the corner of his lips. "I was kind of hoping you'd come find me."

I raised an eyebrow, attempting to maintain an air of indifference despite my racing heart. Interesting? I guess you could call it that. He knew exactly what he was doing last night, being extremely hard to resist. It was infuriating and exhilarating all at once. And to top it off, I had to witness those girls throwing themselves at him.

"Well, you had plenty of attention last night," I said, pushing a loose strand of hair behind my ear and averting my eyes. "And interesting? Is that what you want to call it?" I challenged, crossing my arms over my chest.

"Would you prefer me to be more specific?" Reese teased, turning the boat towards a secluded cove.

"Maybe I would," I shot back defiantly, trying not to let my gaze linger too long on his toned frame. "And then maybe you could be more specific about what the hell we're doing out here."

"Isn't it obvious?" he asked rhetorically, pulling the boat to a stop and cutting the engine. The silence that followed was almost deafening, leaving only the sound of gentle waves. "I'm into you. How much more specific can I be?"

My breath hitched at his admission, but I refused to let him see just how much his words affected me. Instead, I shot him a steely gaze, determined not to fall under his spell so easily.

"You don't even know me," I blurted out, feeling the need to draw a line in the sand. "And you should know that nothing is going to happen between us again." The memory of our previous encounter threatened to surface, but I shook it away.

He's not the type of guy I'd ever picture myself dating. He was arrogant and self-assured, and he probably had no intentions of settling down. He was alluring, I'd give him that—but we lived completely different lives.

Reese's smile broadened into a devilish smirk as he leaned back against the boat railing, his emerald eyes glistening with mischief. "I know... that's another reason we're here. I wanna get to know you," he said, with amusement. "I'll play by your rules."

He paused for a moment, running his fingers through his dark hair before continuing, "But want to know what I think?" I raised an eyebrow, intrigued despite my reservations. He pushed off the railing and leaned in close, his warm breath tickling my ear as he whispered, "I think you're going to have a hard time keeping your hands off me. Before you know it, you'll be begging to kiss me again... probably asking to sit on my face."

His confidence was bordering on arrogance, yet it was undeniably alluring. I felt a flutter between my legs and my pulse raced at his bold statement, but I refused to show any weakness. Instead, I laughed hysterically at his confidence, trying to brush off the weight of his words. Those words that sounded incredibly hot coming out of his mouth.

"You're laughing at me?" Reese asked, smirking in disbelief.

"Your ego," I said, shaking my head. "It's just... very impressive."

"Is it now?" he replied, raising an eyebrow playfully.

"I don't even know how there's room for us to be on the same boat with your ego," I confirmed, unable to suppress a grin.

As I looked over at him, I could no longer keep it suppressed—

the memory of our passionate kiss came flooding back. Thinking about his soft lips against mine sent cold shivers through my body, despite the warm sun shining brightly above us. I scolded myself for even entertaining the thought, but it was becoming harder and harder to ignore.

"At least you think something about me is impressive," Reese replied, his gaze never leaving mine as he maintained a confident grin. "But it's only a matter of time before you realize what a catch I am."

"Keep dreaming," I shot back, trying to ignore the way my skin tingled under the intensity of his stare. As much as I wanted to deny it, there was something about the force drawing me into Reese Carrington that I couldn't control. And it terrified me.

"We'll see about that," he said simply, his eyes glittering with anticipation. He straightened up, giving me some much-needed space as he turned his attention to the glistening waters surrounding the boat.

I exhaled slowly, my pulse gradually returning to normal for a moment. I knew that Reese had planted a seed of doubt in me. Could I really resist the magnetic pull between us?

"Truthfully, you want to know what I like about you, Hartford?" Reese said, breaking the comfortable silence. His eyes were fixed on me.

I raised an eyebrow, letting out a playful smirk. "Let's hear it."

He smiled, shaking his head slightly. "You don't play mind games. You're honest, sometimes maybe too honest, but it's refreshing." Reese's tone was surprisingly sincere.

I looked out over the lake, the tension slightly fading between us. "I've spent so much time playing characters, immersing myself in drama... When I'm not on stage, I just want to be me. I like authenticity."

Reese watched me closely. "Sounds exhausting. Wearing a mask all the time."

"It kind of is," I admitted. "Sometimes it's exhausting and

draining—but in the end, it's all worth it. Just like I'm sure baseball is for you."

"Definitely worth it," he laughed. "Speaking of baseball...I need to hit the batting cages later tonight."

He pulled open a cabinet door to grab his phone to check the time, revealing neatly stacked books that filled the small space to the brim.

"Wow, I didn't take you for the bookish type," I said, unable to keep the surprise out of my tone as I stepped closer.

"There's a lot you don't know about me."

"Apparently," I admitted, crouching down to get a better look. My fingers brushed against the spines of various titles—literature, philosophy, several law books—each book a new layer of Reese Carrington.

"Listen," I said, my voice cheerful with the thrill of this new discovery. "Books are the way to my heart. They're how I travel."

A soft chuckle escaped him. "Is that so? Haven't heard that one before."

"Absolutely. They can take you anywhere you want to go." I explained.

"Noted," he said simply, his smile widened, revealing a rare vulnerability that he usually kept locked away.

I pulled out one of the books on top, my focus shifting as a post-it note slipped from between the pages, fluttering to the floor.

"Oops," I said, bending to pick it up.

"Leave it," he said quickly, but not quickly enough to stop me from seeing the scribbled notes on it.

"Criminal law?" I asked, holding up the slip of paper, noticing that several other bookmarks were peeking out from the book's edge; it was covered with similar neon post-its.

A brief look of vulnerability crossing his face before the mask of confidence returned. "Maybe I'm full of surprises—or maybe I just think the law is interesting," he said with a small smile, taking the note from my hand and tucking it back into the book.

"Maybe there's hope for you after all," I teased, though the realization that Reese might have dreams beyond baseball and the carefree lifestyle he projected struck a chord within me.

I watched him carefully replace the Criminal Law book among the others, the post-it notes now hidden from view. It was then, surrounded by his secret studious world, that I understood that there was more depth and complexity to Reese Carrington.

"Here," he said, handing me a particularly worn volume. "I think you'll appreciate this one."

I glanced down at the worn cover—a vintage edition of 'Hamlet'—and felt an inexplicable throb in my chest. How could he have known? I performed as Ophelia in our last theater production, a role that I was incredibly proud of.

"Hamlet?" My voice echoed a mix of astonishment and curiosity, betraying the surprise that had taken over me. The moment felt heavy, almost as heavy as the leather-bound book I held in my hands.

Reese's smile widened. "Yeah. You strike me as someone who appreciates the classics. The tragedy, the madness—the undying love or whatever."

I knew one thing for certain, this boy was anything but simple—and there were layers to him that went beyond what could be seen on the surface.

thirteen

"HEY, can I try driving the boat?" I asked suddenly, desperate to change the subject and distract myself from the moment we were having.

"Sure," Reese agreed, looking surprised by my request. "Come here."

I walked over to stand next to him, hesitating slightly before placing my hands on the wheel. His proximity sent a flurry of goosebumps across my skin, and I could feel my palms becoming sweaty beneath my grip. His touch was gentle yet firm as he showed me how to steer and maintain our course.

"See? You're a natural," Reese said encouragingly as I navigated the boat through the waves. "I knew you had it in you."

"Thanks," I replied, my cheeks warming with his praise. But beneath the surface, a small part of me still wanted another taste of his lips, and I knew that no amount of laughter or distraction could completely erase the desire. Time would tell if I could resist the pull towards Reese Carrington.

"Hey, so how have you been doing?" I asked tentatively, shifting my gaze from the water to his expression. "I heard you and Blair had a pretty big argument last night."

Reese sighed, running a hand through his tousled hair. "Yeah, we did. But things will be fine. It's just that... we both know this situation isn't going anywhere. We've been dragging it on for too long, and it's time to let it go."

"Is that really what you want?" I questioned, my own heart twisting at the thought of Reese getting back together with her. Despite their tumultuous history, they seemed like such a perfect couple—-the gorgeous boy with the stunning, wealthy girl who always turned heads wherever she went.

"It is what I want," he admitted, his eyes searching mine for a moment before looking away. "But other times, I wonder if it's just easier to do the same shit we've been doing because it's what everyone expects." He shifted uncomfortably, clearly struggling with the vulnerability he was displaying.

"I get it," I offered reassuringly, hoping to ease his discomfort. "But maybe if you stopped trying so hard to please everyone else and do what you want, you'd be happier. And who knows? You might even stop being such a dick most of the time."

His eyes widened in surprise and then narrowed playfully. "Oh, so now I'm a dick?"

"I'm not wrong!" I defended myself with a grin, realizing how much I liked this rare moment when Reese let his guard down and allowed me to see beyond his tough exterior.

"Fair enough," he agreed, smirking. Reese's eyes danced with amusement, and I couldn't help but laugh.

"Hey, I call it like I see it," I said, trying to stifle my giggles.

"Alright, I'll give you that," he said, snickering, his laughter infectious. It felt like a weight had been lifted from both of our shoulders as we shared this light-hearted moment.

"You really should laugh more often and relax, Reese. You're not too terrible when you put your guard down."

"Hartford, are you actually complimenting me right now?" Reese feigned shock, placing a hand over his heart dramatically. "I'm touched."

"Watch it," I warned, unable to suppress my grin. "Or I might take it back."

We spent the rest of the evening making our way around the lake, talking and laughing more than I ever expected. He told me stories from his childhood, like the first time his dad took him to Italy.

"I told my dad I wanted the real deal, and next thing I knew, we were on a flight to Italy." he said nonchalantly.

My mouth fell open, unsure whether to laugh or be jealous. "Just like that? Out of nowhere?"

"Just like that." He nodded, looking proud and a tad sheepish at the same time. "Landed in Rome and had the best pasta of my life by dinner."

"Wow," I breathed out, a mixture of amazement and amusement dancing in my thoughts. "I can't even imagine that. If I told my mom I wanted authentic Italian, she'd toss me an apron and tell me to start boiling the noodles myself."

Reese laughed, an infectious sound that made me smile despite the bright, flashing reminder of how different our worlds were. "Yeah, it's crazy thinking back on it now. My dad... he always tried to make the impossible happen for me when I was younger."

"Must've been nice," I mused, not with envy, but a genuine curiosity for this life that was so different from my own experiences. I was struck by how different he seemed away from everyone else— more relaxed and genuinely charming.

"And what about your mom?" Reese asked, his voice gentle as he raised an eyebrow, "tell me more about her."

Even now, I couldn't help but smile at an act of kindness she did that I'll never forget. "She was a little strict growing up. But I could talk to her about anything. She did something pretty amazing for me once, kind of like my version of Italy."

"Go on," Reese urged, raising an eyebrow with genuine interest.

"My Grandma and I, we used to garden together—she had the most beautiful flowers I've ever seen." The corners of my mouth lifted unconsciously. "It was our thing. After she passed, it felt like a piece of me went with her and all that beauty was gone. But somehow, every time spring rolls around and I see flowers start to bloom, it's like she's still here, you know?"

"Sounds like she meant a lot to you," Reese said softly, holding my gaze with genuine empathy.

"More than I can explain. And Mom—she noticed how much I missed her. One day, she came home with these seeds..." I trailed off, lost in the recollection of the day my mother handed me the tiny packet.

"Seeds?" Reese repeated, his curiosity piqued.

"Rare ones. Himalayan poppy seeds. They were Grandma's favorite. The flowers are this light blue color that you'd swear couldn't exist naturally. Magical almost." It was the only thing I planted since she passed.

"Did they grow?" he asked, leaning in closer.

"Nah," I admitted with a wistful chuckle. "They never bloomed like Grandma's did. And Mom... she could never find those seeds again. But she got me back into the garden—it was special." I glanced up at Reese, meeting his gaze. "Nothing extravagant like your Italy story, though."

Reese pushed off from his seat, closing the distance between us until he was crouched beside me, his presence grounding. "Your story beats mine," he said, his voice earnest.

But before the silence could stretch too long, he straightened up, his charm sliding back into place seamlessly. "Anyway," he said with a wink, his smile returned. "Did you ever hear about the time I convinced Crew and Bailey I was a lost prince?"

I could sense that our discussion was starting to delve into deeper territory and he was trying to retreat. His voice had its usual hint of mischief, but I knew then that he wasn't as carefree as he seemed—even if he hardly ever showed it.

When we got back to the marina, Reese tied up the boat and helped me out onto the dock. As we walked to his truck, our hands brushed against each other as we exchanged playful banter. I could still feel the attraction lingering between us. Even the faint touch stirred something inside me. I glanced at his vehicle, a shiny

black truck with tinted windows and a slightly aggressive stance. It was exactly the kind of truck one would expect from Reese.

"Here we are," he said, opening the tailgate and casually tossing a few of his things into the back. He then walked over to the passenger side, opened the door, and extended a hand to help me in. His green eyes met mine, a silent invitation for me to trust him. His strong grip held on to my hand, guiding me up into the high seat.

I settled into the plush leather seat, my eyes wandering around the interior. It wasn't long before something caught my eye, a CD that was tucked into the otherwise sleek and clutter-free dashboard. I couldn't help but laugh.

"Really? You're a Swiftie?" I asked, teasing him while holding up the CD case so he could see it.

"Can you blame me?" he replied with a lopsided grin that somehow made him even more attractive. "I'm not ashamed to admit that I like her music."

"Neither am I," I admitted, still snickering. "I just wouldn't have expected it from you, that's all, and who even has CDs anymore?" I joked, laughing harder as I dangled the CD just out of Reese's reach. His arm was fully extended, fingertips grazing the case, but I continued to pull it away, my laughter bubbling up with each attempt he made to grab it.

"Give it back," he demanded, shifting over the center console and leaning in closer while still reaching for the CD. My smile faded, knowing how close we were now. I could feel the heat radiating off his body. His eyes were dark and intense, full of desire.

"Reese," I whispered hesitating, barely able to breathe as I stared into those hypnotizing eyes. Our faces were only inches apart, and I knew without a doubt that all it would take was one small movement for our lips to touch.

His gaze drifted to my mouth and lingered there for a heartbeat before he pulled back, as if physically forcing himself to put some distance between us. "Don't worry, I'm playing by your rules, Hartford," A small smile formed at the corner of his mouth, and I had the sudden urge to kiss it away, to explore him further—but I didn't. "Let's get you home."

My stupid, stupid rules. Him respecting my wishes only magnified the desire for him that was consuming me, and I hated how much more I wanted him because of it.

The drive back to the cabin was a blur of teasing remarks and tense glances. When we finally arrived, he walked me to the front door. The air between us thickened with an unspoken energy, and I fidgeted nervously with the keys in my hand.

With his hands stuffed in the pockets of his shorts, he turned to face me and the faint porch light. "Change your mind yet?" His voice broke the silence, playful and sure. "Ready for that goodnight kiss?"

I felt that familiar flutter in my stomach, the one I'd been trying to ignore ever since the first time I met him. I shook my head, trying to brush off the butterflies. "Not a chance."

Reese chuckled and stepped closer, taking my hand in his. My breath caught in my throat as he kissed the back of my hand.

"The pleasure was all mine, Hartford," he said, his voice low and smooth before he let go of my hand.

When he finally walked away, I was left standing on the front porch, disoriented by the sudden absence of his touch. Reese shot me a wink and gave me one last look—a silent communication that this was just the beginning—before turning and walking away into the night.

fourteen

THE TAPPING on my door pulled me from a deep sleep. As I blinked and became aware of the morning light streaming through my window. I could hear Boston's voice from outside my room.

"Hey, you up?" he called out, tapping his knuckles against the wooden surface again.

"Coming," my voice was groggy from sleep as I dragged myself out of bed, shuffling to the door in my pajamas.

I opened the door, revealing him in a white fitted t-shirt and shorts. His hair appeared slightly disheveled as if he had just woken up.

"Hey, Boston... What's up?" I rubbed my eyes with the back of my hand. "It's early."

"We need to talk," he said, with a steady voice. "About Reese."

"Reese?" I frowned, clearly confused. "What about him?"

Boston's jaw tightened for a moment before he spoke. "I saw you last night when we were leaving the restaurant across the street from the lake. You were with Reese."

His tone was casual, but his stance told another story. It felt like there was a silent accusation that lingered in his tone. Maybe he was being protective—but there was also something else, some sort of tension that hadn't been there before.

"Okay...and?" I asked, unable to keep the defensiveness from creeping into my voice. My heart thumped erratically, knowing full well that Reese was the one person he had a problem with, maybe even hated.

"Why did you get in his truck, Chandler?"

"Why do you care, Boston?" I shot back, not sure why my defensive walls were rising up but feeling them there all the same.

Boston's blue eyes turned steely, and he let out a short, humorless laugh. "I don't," he said, his tone clipped. "I just can't understand why you'd waste your time with that arrogant prick."

His words stung, though I wasn't sure if it was because of his jab at Reese or that it felt like he was still holding something back. "Why do you care who I spend my time with?"

Boston shifted, crossing his arms over his chest. His jaw flexed for a moment before he relaxed it. "I don't. You can do what you want."

"Is there something else you want to say, Boston?" I crossed my arms over my chest, demanding honesty.

"I just... I don't trust him," he admitted. "You know what kind of guy he is. And I'm just looking out for you."

"Since when do you get to decide who I spend my time with?" I retorted, my voice edged with irritation. "I'm not a little girl anymore. I can take care of myself."

"Of course you can," he said quickly, running a hand through his hair in what seemed like frustration. "I just want you to be careful."

He never cared before who I spent my time with. Back at home, he never paid attention to what I did. He was always preoccupied—surrounded by his friends, by stunning girls, and all of a sudden now he cared?

"You don't have anything to worry about," I said softly as I looked away. "Maybe he's just misunderstood."

"Uh-huh," he breathed. "I'm sure that's all it is."

"Look," I sighed, meeting his gaze once more. "I appreciate that you care, but trust me, I got this. Okay?"

"Alright," he nodded reluctantly. "I hope you know what you're doing."

"I do," I said, offering a small smile. "Now, can I go back to sleep?"

"Sure," Boston conceded for now, pushing off from the door frame with a shrug. "I'll see you later."

As he turned to leave, I leaned against the door, wondering what that was about and if there was more to it than just Boston looking out for me.

I felt my phone vibrate in my pocket and my heart leaped as Kristina's smiling face popped up on the screen with an incoming FaceTime call. Without hesitation, I swiped to answer, already bubbling with anticipation.

"Finally!" I exclaimed, unable to keep the giddiness from my voice.

"Chandler! I don't have long." Kristina's voice rushed out, breathless as she was walking quickly. "But it's been incredible here. Like a dream. And don't you worry, I've been taking notes, so I can bring you back all my new acting tips!"

"Tell me everything going on with you," she beamed, her eyes sparkling with that same infectious energy I always knew. "Any new cute boys?"

"Where do I even start?" I laughed, knowing there wouldn't be enough time to explain. "There's been so much happening. And... yes, but it's complicated."

"Wait, you mean a cute boy besides Boston?" Kristina teased, a knowing glint dancing in her eyes.

"Surprisingly, yes." I could feel my cheeks warm as she was putting me on the spot.

"Ooh, do tell," Kristina prodded, but before I could delve into the details, her expression shifted to one of mild regret.

"Shoot, I've got to get back to it, Chan. But we'll catch up properly soon, promise," she said, her words tinged with the faintest hint of longing.

"Fine, but I'm holding you to that," I tilted my head, giving her a serious look, wishing we had more time.

"Aw, I really miss you," Kristina sighed, her sentiment echoing through the miles that stretched between us.

"Miss you more." I sighed. Her words were like a breath of fresh air, and hearing from her always made my day brighter.

Later that evening, the sun dipped low in the sky, casting long shadows across the baseball field as Boston gripped the bat tightly in his hands. My parents sat in the stands next to me eagerly watching.

"Strike!" The umpire's voice cut through the haze like a knife, and I realized he just missed the first pitch.

"Come on, bro, you got this," Parker called out encouragingly from the dugout as he readied himself for the next pitch.

The ball soared through the air, and he swung. The satisfying crack of the bat connected with the ball and I was relieved for a moment until I watched it fly straight into the left fielder's glove.

"Shit." I sighed as I watched him walk back toward the dugout, looking pissed at his performance.

I spotted Reese in the dugout, propped against the fence with a smirk on his face, and Boston heading straight toward him.

"What the hell is your problem?" Boston shouted, throwing off his helmet and tossing his bat aside.

"My problem? Nah. I think you're the one with the problem." Reese jeered. "I think you can't handle the pressure that comes with being on this team. You should probably save yourself the embarrassment and quit."

"Shut up, Reese," Boston growled, stepping closer to him. His fist was clenched, as if resisting the urge to punch him in the face.

"Or what?" Reese shot back, shoving Boston forcefully in the chest. Boston's restraint snapped, and he shoved him back even harder.

Parker, and two of their teammates, Bailey and Crew, rushed in, pulling Reese and Boston away from each other before it could escalate further, but they were both still trying to push through to get to each other.

"Enough!" Coach Levy roared, storming over to them with a furious expression. His dark hair was damp with sweat, sticking to his forehead as he stood between them. "I don't know what the fuck is going on between you two, but if you ever bring it to the field again, I'll replace you both without a second thought! Understood?"

"Understood," Boston responded, avoiding his piercing glare. Reese stayed silent, his jaw clenched, and his eyes still locked onto Boston's.

"Good," Coach Levy nodded with a stern expression. "Now get the hell out of my sight. You're both done."

I watched from the bleachers, my heart raced as Boston and Reese were thrown out of the game. Boston's usually happy-go-lucky face was tight with frustration. His piercing blue eyes were now stormy. Reese just smirked and tossed the ball up in the air, catching it with carefree ease.

"What just happened?" Dad's voice was rough with disbelief as he rose to his feet, every line of his body rigid with frustration.

"Not again," Mom added, her lips pressed into a thin line. She always had a way of saying so much with so little. Her disappointment was obvious.

I watched them navigate their way through the sea of legs, making a beeline toward Boston.

The scene that unfolded before me tore open a memory, the one I knew Mom had remembered as well. Boston was up to bat while Reese was pitching on the other team a few summers back.

* * *

"Strike him out, Reese!" someone had shouted from the dugout, their words slicing through the humid summer air.

"Come on, Boston, show him what you've got!" my dad called

out, but his encouragement was drowned in the jeers from the other team.

Reese wound up, and with a swift motion, he sent the ball spinning towards home plate. Boston swung with all he had, but the crack of the bat never came—only the slap of the ball hitting the catcher's mitt. Strike three. Boston's shoulders slumped as he turned away from the plate.

Reese and a couple of his teammates heckled Boston, laughing and saying remarks I couldn't quite hear from where I was sitting.

After the game, Parker and Boston were gathering their things and several players, including Reese, approached them from the other team.

"Watch where you're going," one of them said to Boston.

Boston clenched his fists. "You need to get out of my face."

"Or what?" Reese took a threatening step toward him. "You gonna do something about it?"

That was it. Boston launched himself at Reese, taking him to the ground. They went at it, rolling in the dirt. Parker and the rest of their teammates quickly jumped in. Soon it was an all-out brawl between both teams.

Fists flew as both sides exchanged blows. Coaches and parents rushed over to break up the chaos. When they were finally separated, Boston stood breathing hard, his uniform covered in dust and dirt. Reese glared at him, his nose was bleeding.

"This isn't over," he spat as he was pulled away.

They were rivals on the baseball field from that moment forward.

Watching them now, both being forced to leave the game, brought those old emotions bubbling up to the surface. It was more than just a game for them—it became a competition and a rivalry that had only grown fiercer with time.

fifteen

I COULD SEE Boston still focused on the game, standing close to the field but far enough back to stay off the coach's radar. I saw Reese cut a determined path toward the practice field, in the opposite direction—and couldn't help but wonder where he was going. The final inning passed in a blur and my parents barely noticed when I told them I needed to go, but I'd see them at the next game. Their concern was still on Boston. "Sure, honey," Mom said absently, her attention focused on my dad and their conversation, allowing me to slip away.

The practice field was empty and more silent than I expected, even though it was just a short distance from the large crowd that was now leaving the game. The sunlight was fading, and I found myself drawn to the rhythmic clinking sound interrupting the quiet. It was the unmistakable noise of a baseball bat connecting with pitch after pitch.

"Carrington?" The word slipped out of my mouth before I could see inside the cage. There was no response, but there didn't need to be. It had to be him.

Reese was deep in concentration, his every muscle coiled and released with each swing. "Why do you always have to throw jabs at

Boston?" I called out, trying to get his attention as I watched him take another powerful swing. "What's it going to take for you two to just get along?"

His shoulders tensed ever so slightly at the question, but he didn't look at me. Instead, his gaze remained locked on the pitching machine, and then the clack of the bat met another ball.

I pushed open the gate to the batting cage. The metallic creak was louder than I expected. The sound of the machine tirelessly serving up fastballs continued.

"Answer me, you ass." My voice echoed slightly in the enclosed space as I began my rant. "Help me understand. And don't you care what anyone thinks? The MLB could want nothing to do with you now for getting kicked out of the game."

Finally, Reese stopped. "He tried to pick a fight with me," he responded, his voice carrying a casual tone. He dropped the bat on the floor, leaning it against the chain-link of the cage as he walked toward me. He cocked his head to the side, stepping in close and shielding me from the next ball that was released, which thudded harmlessly against the netting beside us.

His proximity was unsettling, yet thrilling, the air filled with an energy that seemed unique to whenever we occupied the same space. Our gazes held, and for a moment, the world outside, the argument that just happened with him and Boston—all of it faded into the background.

His green eyes blazed with that familiar defiant spark, which sent my pulse racing. He stood so close I could feel the heat emanating from his body, smell his woodsy scent mixed with leather clinging to him. "And no, I don't care what anyone thinks," he said with that cocky grin. "I'm the best pitcher in college baseball right now."

"And get out of the cage," he growled. "You could get hit by the fucking ball." His tone was sharp, a clear warning, but I stood my ground.

His words were bold and unapologetic. I swallowed hard, my

mind no longer able to concentrate on the reason I had entered the cage, only on my heightened awareness of him.

My heart beat a frantic rhythm against my chest as if it was trying to keep pace with the adrenaline that was rushing through me. "Well," I started, my voice steadier than I felt, "your attitude could still ruin it."

He smirked as if he knew a secret the rest of the world didn't. "I can convince them I'm worth it," he said with a quiet confidence that didn't match his earlier cockiness.

"God, you're so infuriating," I whispered. But even as the frustration bubbled inside me, I could still feel the undeniable pull—that strong, annoyingly present force that seemed to draw me in despite my better judgment.

Without another word, Reese closed the space between us. His breath was sweet from the gum he'd been chewing and it mingled with mine as he pressed me against the fence. His body was hard and his heartbeat throbbed as I felt the tautness of his stomach and hips, pressing into me.

He shifted his position slightly, giving me a glimpse of the raw desire burning in his eyes. With a decisive pull—I snatched his jersey, and brought him in close. His teeth caught my bottom lip, biting ever so slightly in a tantalizing motion, drawing me in before his lips crashed against mine.

There was nothing gentle or careful about this kiss. It was demanding, taking everything he desired without hesitation— leaving me breathless. His lips continued to move with a relentless hunger that felt like it was stripping away all the layers of his hard exterior, revealing something raw and needy beneath. He was addicting. Kissing him was all-consuming and devouring, as if he needed me to understand without words that he wanted every inch of me—and nothing else mattered.

He groaned as his hands began exploring the curve of my waist before sliding up under my shirt to caress my bare skin. The rough pads of his fingers circling the sensitive peaks of my breasts sent jolts of pleasure coursing through my body.

He continued to kiss me as his hands curved my waist again before they slid further down to my ass, his fingers pressing firmly yet tenderly as if claiming every part he touched as his own territory. He tightened his grip, effortlessly lifting me off the ground as my legs wrapped around him.

The intensity between us was overwhelming—the heat of his body on mine, the rough texture of his uniform against my skin, and the sweet taste of him on my tongue.

He held me in the air and continued to kiss me. Then, with ease and careful control, Reese carried me, stepping out of the batting cage and slowly lowered me down on the solid ground just outside.

My breath was still uneven as I pulled away from him, just barely. Still confused, I locked eyes with his—searching for an answer in his fiery gaze. "I just don't understand what the deal is with Boston."

His expression darkened instantly, the name hanging heavy between us like a sudden storm cloud. "Don't fucking say his name when you're kissing me," he spat out, his voice low and dangerous.

Reese backed away, his hands releasing me as if I'd scorched him. The wind hit my flushed skin, and I was no longer in the warmth of his embrace. He walked back into the batting cage, his movements rigid. The sound of the gate slamming shut echoed through the air, final and unyielding.

"And don't fucking walk in here again when the machine is on," he said, now deceptively calm. He then grabbed his bat, separating us from the moment we just had.

Silence hung heavy as I stood there, the taste of him lingering on my lips, and the sting of him releasing me. I crossed my arms and took determined steps away from the cage.

"YOU'RE INFURIATING!" I yelled without looking back. My heart pounded, each beat a reminder of all the emotions he just stirred within me. "And I said his name AFTER I was kissing you!" I added.

I made it only a few steps before curiosity—and something deeper, something stubborn—compelled me to glance over my shoulder. Reese had taken up his bat again and was waiting for the next pitch. His stance was relaxed. But it wasn't him acting like nothing just happened that floored me—it was the slight smile I could almost see playing on his lips as the bat connected with the ball.

sixteen

I TRUDGED HOME, my shoes scraping against the pavement with each weary step. It felt like I had been walking for hours, even though the ball field was only a mile from Boston's cabin. I knew that fight with Boston and Reese probably had everything to do with me, but I wasn't ready to face Boston, so I walked slowly to have some time alone with my thoughts.

When I finally arrived, I found Parker and Boston's gear strewn across the front porch. Their grass-stained uniforms laid over the railing, baseball bags were tossed on the floor, and their gloves sat on the patio bench.

With a sigh, I sank into the bench and picked up Boston's mitt, running my fingers over the worn leather. As I did, my eyes widened, and I froze in place when I noticed a faded friendship bracelet tied into the stitching on the inside of the mitt, its threads loose and frayed. I recognized the bracelet instantly. I had given it to Boston years ago when we were just kids—the first time we had ever met.

My mind started racing, and my heart suddenly pounded. Boston had kept it all this time? I had assumed he would have lost it years ago. I mean, I was five years old, but clearly, it still meant something to him.

What does this mean? The faded bracelet consumed my thoughts. Then I heard the front door open and the porch lights turned on. I quickly tucked away the mitt as Boston and Parker stepped onto the porch. "There you are. Where have you been?" Parker asked, eyeing me skeptically.

"I wanted to walk home, needed the fresh air," I said with a shrug, trying to sound casual.

Boston gave me a long look before giving me a faint smile and rummaging through his equipment. Then he took his mitt and quickly shoved it below a pile of items.

"So," I began hesitantly, "what happened tonight?"

"Boston almost beat Reese's ass, that's what." Parker smirked, as he began to pick up his items to take them inside. Then he shut the door behind him—leaving me alone with Boston.

Boston sat down next to me and let out a long sigh. "It was all on me," he confessed, running a hand through his wavy hair. "I just let stress get the best of me. I never would have forgiven myself if they lost."

"Boston," I said firmly, gripping his hand for emphasis, "Being on this team could lead you somewhere big. You can't let anything get in the way of that. I don't know how many times I've heard you say that you're going to use baseball to give your mom a better life. You talked about it since we were kids."

His jaw clenched, and I could see the weight of my words sinking in. He nodded slightly, knowing that I was right. We sat there silently, hands still intertwined for a moment before he spoke. "I know, it won't happen again. I was just off today." He squeezed my hand reassuringly before letting go.

"Anyway, I gotta go take a shower." He grimaced, realizing how sweaty he still was from the game. With a small smile and a wink, he turned and walked toward the front door.

Just as his hand touched the doorknob, I found my voice.

"Hey, Boston?"

He paused and turned back to look at me. Even with the porch light's dim glow, I could still make out the curiosity in his eyes.

"Was it because of me?" I asked, my voice barely above a whisper. "Did you get into it with Reese because of me?"

I knew him well enough to know that even if it was, Boston would never say it. He was too humble—not ever the type of person to blame someone else for his actions.

There was a pause, a moment of hesitation, where I saw something flicker behind those cautious blue depths. Then, almost effortlessly, he shook his head.

"No," he lied. "It wasn't about you."

The air seemed to grow heavy with his denial, and I found myself searching his face for the truth that I felt certain was being withheld as I waited for him to break the silence.

"This shit with me and Reese goes way back, you know that. To the very first summer I started coming here for baseball. It's just the way we are," he added, but the tightness in his voice, the way his gaze couldn't quite meet mine, told me all I needed to know. I didn't believe him—not for a second.

"Okay, Boston."

I watched him go and let out a breath I didn't know I was holding. Part of me wanted to stop him again, to ask about the bracelet that was now tugging at my heart. I wanted to ask him why he kept it for so long, why it was in his glove, but something held me back. Maybe it was fear of what the answers might be if he actually opened up to me—or the uncertainty of things changing. What if it didn't mean anything, and he kept it because I was like a little sister to him? That might hurt more than anything else.

Instead, I stayed silent like a coward, as the darkness began to consume me. The shadows grew longer, wrapping around me like a cold blanket. I hugged my knees to my chest, lost in thought.

Have Boston's feelings toward me changed? And if they did, what would that mean? I had never thought about the possibility of us becoming something—mostly, because I didn't think he'd ever see me in that way. I mean, he was my first crush, and I adored him—it's Boston, how could I not? But I was probably overthinking all of this. Boston was still the same person he'd always been. I was just jumping to conclusions. Still, I couldn't stop myself from thinking about him in a new light. No matter how much I wanted to deny it, things felt different between us now.

seventeen

IT WAS FINALLY the Fourth of July, the only downside being that it was going to be one of the hottest days so far. I quickly pulled my wavy hair up into a clip to keep it off my neck and threw on a loose t-shirt over my swimsuit before I made my way outside to the dock.

The water was smooth and reflected the hovering trees and blue sky so perfectly it was hard to tell where one ended and the other began. I dangled my feet in the warm water, watching the sun dance across the lake, lost in thought.

But the calm was quickly interrupted.

"Shouldn't you be sleeping in or something?" Boston asked as he came into view, trudging toward me on the dock.

"Could ask you the same," I countered as I looked back at him—all broad shoulders and annoyingly handsome.

"And miss out on this view?" he winked. "Never."

"I'm flattered," I joked, pushing a few strands of hair out of my face. "You just can't resist my company."

"Guilty," Boston admitted as he sat down beside me, his shoulder just barely touching mine. His presence was a blend of comfort and unease. He stretched out his long legs, mirroring my position, and we both stared out at the water for a moment.

I had been avoiding him, still unsure of how to feel about the bracelet. But I knew I couldn't continue like this forever, always wondering and avoiding my real feelings when it came to him. It was time to step out of my comfort zone and take a risk, even if it meant being vulnerable and in the spotlight of my own life.

"Why did you keep it all these years?" I blurted out.

I glanced over at him, taking in his windswept hair and the strong line of his jaw, unsure of where this was going. I knew I had to finally face my childhood crush, whether it would lead to rejection or it would change everything between us.

He raised an eyebrow. "Keep what?"

"The bracelet. The one I gave you when we were kids." I was hardly able to get the words out, almost too afraid of what his answer was going to be.

Boston met my gaze, his sky-colored eyes searching mine. His jaw tightened, and he seemed to weigh every word that was about to come. "I've just held onto it since the day we first met," he said, carefully.

"So..." I began, searching for the right words. "Does the bracelet mean something to you?"

Boston looked down, rubbing the back of his neck with his hand. "Of course it does."

"Why?" I pressed. "Why would you keep it?"

He was quiet for a long moment before responding. "You know your brother is my best friend, right? I'd never wanna cross a line with him—or your parents, for that matter. They treat me like one of their own."

He trailed off, his expression conflicted, like he was trying to let me down easy. I felt my heart sink. I guess part of me hoped that he felt the same way about me that I've always felt about him. But now I knew that was never the case.

"It's okay," I said softly, giving his hand a squeeze before letting it go. "You don't have to explain anything else. I get it."

Boston looked like he wanted to say more, but he just nodded silently. We sat on the dock a little longer. The space between us felt wider than ever.

I wasn't just hurt because he was letting me down but I could tell that even after I was vulnerable with him, that he was still holding something back, and I wasn't sure what it was but I knew that he wasn't being completely honest.

He stood and offered me his hand. "C'mon, we should head back. I'll make us breakfast."

After a moment, I took it, allowing him to pull me up. We walked back down the dock together, but things felt different. We both felt it.

After breakfast, I went to Willow's and stormed into her room, collapsing dramatically onto her bed while explaining what had just happened with Boston.

Willow's eyes went wide. "No way. Boston had the bracelet this whole time?"

"Yes!" I shouted, sitting up. "I saw it tied into his baseball glove. Can you believe it? He kept it all these years and never said anything."

Willow gave me a knowing look. "So what does this mean?"

I sighed, flopping back down onto the mountain of pillows. "I don't know. He didn't really explain what it meant. He basically just said he's Parker's best friend, so he'd never go there. And I have this thing starting up with Reese now, anyway."

"Right, how could I forget?" Willow said with a smirk.

"I know he's trouble, and I shouldn't do it, but there's just this connection between us, you know? I think I need to see where it goes."

Willow nodded sympathetically. "Yeah, I get it. Just follow your heart and it'll all work out how it's supposed to. I mean, both are hot, and baseball studs—you can't go wrong with either."

I smiled at her gratefully, feeling a bit better. "You always know just what to say."

My phone buzzed with a new text message. I picked it up from Willow's nightstand to see who it was.

Reese: Boat day? Best way to watch the fireworks. And yes, you can bring Willow.

"Reese just invited us on his boat," I said, trying to force a smile.

Willow sat up, intrigued. "Perfect timing... let's do it!"

I didn't hate the idea of Reese's arm around me as we watched the fireworks. A welcome distraction from everything swirling in my head about Boston.

"This is just what I need," I said with a contented sigh as I hit send on the text to Reese, letting him know we'd be there.

Willow gave me an approving nod. "I have just the swimsuit for this little soiree."

The sun sparkled off the calm gray water as I stepped from the dock onto Reese's sleek white boat. He held his hand out to steady me, a dimple flashed in his cheek as he smiled and said, "Welcome aboard, Hartford."

Willow followed behind me and Reese helped her on the boat. Some of his friends were already lounging on the seats at the bow, with drinks in their hands.

Reese grabbed two bottles from the cooler and handed me one. "Cheers," he said, clinking his bottle against mine. I took a sip, enjoying the fizzy sweetness.

"Thanks for inviting us today," I told him.

"Anytime," he replied. "I thought we could all use a little sunshine and relaxation."

Willow cranked up the music and I found myself enjoying the melody, swept up in the playful mood. With the sun on my face and the peaceful water all around, I felt lighter than I had in a while. Maybe this day out on the boat was exactly what I needed.

After we tied up to a row of other boats in a nearby cove, Reese set his drink down and took my hand, pulling me toward the back of the boat.

"Let's get away for a sec," he said, offering me his hand with a daring smile.

"Lead the way," I said, my voice slightly shaky as I steadied myself. Reese flashed his annoyingly handsome smile, guiding me to sit at the stern of the boat. We sat with our feet dangling in the warm water.

Despite the others on the boat, it felt as though they were worlds away as I sat there with Reese. The ease with which we connected, the effortless conversation that flowed between us, made it seem like time stood still.

"Can I ask you something?" I wondered, suddenly curious to know more about him.

"I guess," he responded, genuine interest flickering through his eyes.

"Tell me more about you, about your family," I said, searching for his expression.

Reese's eyes darted away from mine as soon as the words left my mouth, and then he scratched the back of his neck.

"Why do you want to know about my family?" he asked, dodging the question.

I wasn't going to let him get away with being vague. "I want to know where you come from. Tell me about your parents. What are they like?"

Reese hesitated, the smile fading from his face. "My dad is always working. And...I don't really like talking about it, but my mom left when I was a baby. My dad said she couldn't handle how much their life changed from expensive restaurants and parties to staying in and taking care of a baby."

I felt sadness and guilt tightening around my heart as I absorbed the weight of his words. It had been easy to think his life was perfect, because nothing seemed to bother him, but I knew he must have been hurting. Every boy needed his mother, and I couldn't imagine how a mother could ever leave their child. I squeezed his hand understandingly as he shared his pain over his broken family.

"And this pendant necklace I always wear," He looked down, his voice softening. "My dad says it belonged to her." His thumb caressed the pendant. "I don't even remember her, really. But wearing this... it's like a connection to her or something. Maybe the only one."

"And my stepmom..." He trailed off, shaking his head.

I traced the tip of my fingers along the veins on his arm, trying to be consoling, while waiting for him to continue talking.

With a sigh, Reese met my gaze again. "She tries her best to be a mom. She's a great one to my little sister, but they're always traveling with my dad for work. He represents high-profile clients, so they're never in one place for long. I get random texts or calls from her saying they're in Prague or Milan or wherever." He gave a bitter laugh. "Sometimes they're gone for weeks at a time."

My heart ached for him. No wonder he kept everyone at arm's length.

"I'm sorry," I said softly. "That must be really hard."

"It is what it is." Reese's voice was thick with emotion. "I'm used to it by now and spend most of my time on baseball, anyway."

He quickly composed himself, the casual mask slipping back into place. But I had glimpsed the real Reese underneath—lonely, hurting, in need of love. I gently squeezed his hand, hoping he knew he wasn't alone.

We sat there for a moment as the waves rocked the boat gently. He pulled me against his chest. I could feel his heart beating steadily against mine. Reese's hand came up to cradle my face, his thumb grazing my cheek. Slowly, he leaned in, and I thought for a moment he was going to kiss me, but then he pulled back.

"So listen, the Bayside Ball is coming up in a month," he began as his expression turned serious.

I nodded, my stomach fluttering nervously. Willow said the

Bayside Ball was the biggest event of the summer but I hadn't really thought too much about it.

"Yeah?" I said, trying to sound casual.

"I am kind of in search of a date. Someone who can handle the whispers and bullshit that comes with being on my arm." he laughed. "I can't promise you'll have a good time and I know you don't think it sounds that fun, but there's usually never a dull moment with me."

The directness of his request, his smooth charm, sent an unexpected jolt through me.

"Carrington, are you asking me to be your date to the ball?" I asked, needing to hear him say it, to confirm that this wasn't just him messing with me.

"Only if you say yes," he said with a half smile.

eighteen

"REALLY? You want me to be your date?" I asked in disbelief. Reese snickered.

"Why wouldn't I? Come on Hartford, you must know how I feel about you by now." He cupped my face in his hands. "I like you and I want to show you off."

My heart swelled, and I threw my arms around his neck. "Fine, I'll go with you, but I am not wearing a princess dress!"

"You can wear this swimsuit for all I care. You'll be a knockout," he said, smirking at me.

I couldn't stop smiling, still stunned that he asked me to go with him. Out of all the girls in this town that would be dying to go. Although, I couldn't help but compare Reese's openness with Boston's confusing and guarded demeanor lately. It felt like Boston was always holding something back, leaving me grasping for answers. Speaking to Reese, however, felt like a breath of fresh air— he said exactly what he wanted and didn't hold back, and I kind of loved that about him.

"Are you two lovebirds ever going to join the party?" Crew's voice yelled across the boat, shattering the moment between Reese and me. His mischievous grin was evident even from a distance as he waved his drink in the air.

I glanced over at the rest of our friends, who were chatting with others on the boat tied up next to ours while lounging on colorful floats in the water. The sun reflected off the gentle waves, casting a shimmering glow on everyone.

"Guess we should join the others," Reese murmured, his eyes lingering on mine for just a moment longer before he offered me his hand. I placed mine in his, feeling the warmth of his touch, and we made our way back toward the group.

"Finally!" Crew exclaimed once we were within reach, wrapping an arm around Reese and pulling him away.

As we joined them, I couldn't help but notice a few girls on the boat next to ours giving me dirty looks. My heart sank a little, but I knew that saying yes to going to the Bayside Ball with Reese would come with its fair share of jealousy and resentment just like this. It was no secret that practically every girl in town had a thing for Reese. And now here I was, ordinary Chandler Hartford, scoring the hottest date. I steeled myself, remembering that I could handle it.

Reese wrapped a towel around my shoulders, and one of the girls nearby glared at me before tossing her hair and turning away. I hid a smile, thinking of the ridiculousness of their envy.

The engine's low growl subsided as we glided smoothly up to the dock, Reese's boat reflecting the kaleidoscope of colors still lingering in the night sky from the fireworks. Around us, other boats bobbed gently on the water, filled with others who had watched the show, leaning back with drinks in hand.

"You were right. Fireworks are much better on the lake," I confessed, watching Reese expertly tie the boat off.

"The only way to watch," he replied, shooting me that half-smirk I was beginning to grow fond of. He straightened up, surveying the scene with those hypnotic green eyes.

It was then that they came strolling down the dock—a couple of baseball players I recognized from another team that the Blue Devils had just defeated. It seemed evident they had indulged in both the fireworks display and an excess of alcohol. Their laughter was loud and obnoxious.

"Look who it is," one sneered, nudging his buddy. "Reese Carrington, playing captain of daddy's boat."

"Must be nice, having everything handed to you on a silver platter," another added, his tone was dark.

Reese didn't so much as flinch. His carefree demeanor remained undisturbed, but it felt like there might be a storm brewing just under the surface of his calm.

"Jealousy's a bad look on you, boys," Reese responded, his voice laced with a subtle challenge that was nearly imperceptible.

"Easy for you to say," the first guy shot back, taking a step closer, his eyes scanning over Reese's boat. "We don't just get handed a starting position either, we have to earn it."

Reese let out a gentle laugh, unaffected as if their words were nothing he hadn't heard before. It was that dangerous charisma that drew me to him, that made me want to know the man behind the mystery, to uncover the depths hidden beneath the surface. But for those who dared to cross him, I was worried about what was underneath.

"Must really burn you up inside," Reese said, his voice never rising above a casual tone. He stood there and I could almost see a hint of a smile on his face.

"Bet you need daddy to fight your battles for you too," another taunted, voice laced with ridicule. It was then that their eyes landed on me. I had been quietly watching from the boat, with my arms crossed protectively over my chest.

"Hey, look at this one," one jeered, pointing at me with a malicious grin. "Money sure buys pretty company."

"Leave her the fuck out of it," Reese said, his voice taking on a harder edge, but still eerily composed. The atmosphere shifted, and it felt like everyone watching held their breath.

"Or what?" one man challenged, stepping even closer.

Reese's response was not in words. With a calm that was more terrifying than any display of anger, he began to peel off his shirt, revealing his upper body crafted by more than just baseball—probably hours of working out. The motion was unhurried and deliberate, and it wasn't until the fabric slid off his arms and dropped to the deck that I saw the moment of realization in their eyes, indicating they had just pushed the limit too far and made a grave miscalculation.

In a fluid movement too quick to fully grasp, Reese moved closer to the one who made that comment and his right hook connected with his jaw. The sound of impact was sharp. The guy's head snapped backward from the force of the blow, and for a moment, everything seemed to freeze—the crowd, the other boats, the gentle lap of water against the dock—all the other noise stopped.

"Reese, stop!" I called out. I should have been appalled, should have been thinking of ways to pull Reese out of this mess, but all I could focus on was how he captivated me. him, his body—the defined ridges on his perfectly sculpted abs, and the deep lines that seemed to trail down and disappear into his waistband.

"Just need a second!" Reese shouted without looking at me, his entire focus on the two trying to overwhelm him. The second one joined his friend in what seemed like a coordinated effort to try to take Reese down. But Reese sidestepped, deflecting blows.

"Guys, break it up!" Crew's commanding voice cut through the commotion. He and Bailey muscled their way through the gathering crowd. They pulled Reese away and separated from the fight.

"Easy now," Bailey said, his tone light but firm as he held one of them away at arm's length.

"Having fun without us?" Crew joked, though his eyes were serious as he assessed the situation.

Reese straightened up, brushing a hand through his dark hair as if there was nothing to see. "Wouldn't dream of it," he replied with a smirk, looking at his friends as the surrounding tension began to dissipate.

"Man, you're crazy," Bailey said, shaking his head but grinning all the same.

"Come on, let's get out of here before it gets worse," Crew suggested, glancing around at everyone starting to whisper.

"Sure thing," Reese agreed, his smile never wavering. He walked over to me, extending a hand as though I had been through something myself. "You okay?"

"Fine," I said, accepting his hand, feeling the warmth of his palm against mine. His grip was steady, reassuring. I tried not to think about how that same hand had just been clenched in a fist, how it seemed capable of both tenderness and destruction.

"Let's get outta here," Reese said, and there was a lightness in his voice that contrasted the intensity of the moments before. As we left the chaos behind, I couldn't shake the disquieting thoughts in my head—this man inexplicably drew me in.

nineteen

I WALKED up the shadowed path to the cabin. It was late, which meant I could almost picture Parker inside, sunk deep into the living room couch, eyes glued to whatever reality show he denies actually liking.

I was intent on slipping unnoticed through the front door. I didn't feel like talking to Parker about being with Reese today. But as I got closer, I heard the unmistakable sound of laughter, halting me mid-step. And then, the voices grew clearer, and I saw them. Boston and Parker were lounging on the outdoor furniture out front. Caroline was sitting comfortably on Boston's lap—her laughter was high-pitched and forced. Caroline's friend, Sam, that I had met briefly at Reese's first party, sat close to Parker. The soft glow of the string lights above them created a warm and romantic atmosphere, and I didn't want to intrude.

"Seriously," Parker said, his voice carrying a playful edge, "the girls back at college say Boston here is a golden retriever."

"What does that even mean?" I heard Boston ask, as the others snickered.

"Oh, it's a good thing, trust me." Caroline added, playfully.

Hoping not to be seen, I held my breath and slowly tried to slip past them and make my way to the side of the cabin. If I could just make it to the back door, I'd avoid detection, and be in the clear.

"Almost there..." I whispered under my breath. One step, two steps—

Crack! The sound of the branch under my foot was sharp, a break that echoed through the night. Four sets of eyes glanced in my direction in unison, locking onto me like I was under a spotlight.

"Look what the cat dragged in," Parker quipped, his grin visible even in the dim light. Caroline adjusted her posture a bit and remained comfortable on his lap, but her curious gaze remained.

"Chandler!" Boston called out warmly. "Come join us."

Caroline's expression instantly morphed into a scowl. I saw her grip tighten on Boston ever so slightly, and I couldn't help but be a little annoyed at her possessiveness.

"Hi, guys," I said hesitantly, clearly unsure of my welcome. "Sorry, to interrupt—I'm exhausted. Gonna head to bed," stifling a yawn for effect.

"Come on, sis," Parker chimed in, his warm, brotherly love evident in his voice. "Grab a drink and come relax."

"Next time!" I inched toward the door, trying to slip past them with a small smile.

Boston's face fell briefly but quickly recovered, giving a nod. "Alright, get some rest. We'll catch up tomorrow."

I silently twisted the door handle, easing it open just enough to slip through. I took a deep breath before getting myself ready for bed.

The next morning, I rubbed my eyes and stretched, yawning, as I swung my legs over the side of the bed. With a deep breath, I pushed myself up and headed toward the bathroom to take a shower.

I didn't expect to bump into Boston in the hallway so early. He stood there, with a white towel barely covering his waist. His damp, wavy hair hung loosely around his face, and I could smell his body wash—a mix of soap and cedar.

"Uh, sorry," I stammered, realizing that my eyes had lingered on his abs a little too long. "I was just on my way to shower."

"No worries," he smiled, moving to try to slip past me.

Things hadn't been the same between us since I asked him about the bracelet, and I was sort of avoiding him.

"Hey Chandler," he called out. I hesitated, then turned back toward him, curious.

"Have you heard about the Bayside Ball coming up in a few weeks?"

"Uh, yeah," I replied, tucking a strand of damp hair behind my ear. "Reese asked me to go with him."

"Reese?" He asked quietly.

I watched him closely, trying to decipher his thoughts.

"I mean... I think you could find a way better date than him, but that's great—if that's what you want, Chandler," he whispered. "I'm still deciding if I'm going to go."

My gaze lingered on him for a moment longer, my eyes softened with empathy. We stood there in the hallway, caught in a fragile moment. We both didn't know how to handle whatever was going on between us.

"You should go," I finally said, breaking the silence. "You should be there for the awards."

He nodded and looked at me, his face flickering with some unreadable emotion. I hesitated for a moment before turning, taking small steps toward the bathroom. As I reached the door, I paused, glancing back at him. "You know," I said softly, "I'm sure Caroline is hoping you'll ask her. You should take her."

"Caroline?" he echoed. "She is nice and all, but..." he trailed off, forcing a smile. "She's not exactly who I pictured going with, but I'll think about it."

My expression shifted, the corners of my lips curving into a gentle smile that would show more than I could ever say out loud. But instead, here we were, tiptoeing around each other in the hallway, struggling to find our footing.

"Okay," I murmured, nodding my head slowly. "I think she'd

really appreciate it, Boston. You're a great guy—anyone would be lucky to go with you."

My words were meant to comfort him, but I'm unsure if they had the desired effect.

"Thanks, Chandler," he replied, nodding appreciatively. "That means a lot."

As I slipped into the bathroom and closed the door softly behind me, I looked in the mirror at myself, feeling more confused than ever before.

Suddenly, I heard Parker's loud voice from outside the door. "Hey, did I just hear you talking about taking Caroline to the ball?" he asked Boston. I could hear mischief in his voice. "Think they'll allow me to take more than one date?"

I felt a laugh bubble up in my throat, eventually spilling out into the open. I cracked the door slightly and shook my head at Parker.

"Who are these lucky ladies?" I teased, my voice lighter than it had been just moments ago. "And how do you plan on juggling them all night?"

Parker drew a look of deep contemplation, rubbing his chin thoughtfully. "Well, first off, there's Amara from the coffee shop—great sense of humor. And then, of course, there's Kasie from the gym—very athletic, obviously," he said, ticking off names on his fingers. "And let's not forget about Willow."

"Okay, okay, we get it," Boston interjected, rolling his eyes playfully. "You're quite the ladies' man."

"Indeed," he agreed with a dramatic sigh. "It's both a gift and a curse, my friends."

twenty

MY MOM, Willow, and I stepped into the brightly lit boutique, the scent of vanilla and freshly ironed silk enveloping us. Rows of shimmering dresses in every color greeted us as we made our way to the back of the store.

"Oh Chandler, look at this one!" Willow held up a lavender gown, her blue eyes glowing with excitement. "This would look gorgeous with your hair."

I smiled, appreciating her enthusiasm. Dress shopping wasn't my favorite activity, but I knew how much this meant to my mom. And if I was being honest, the thought of walking into the ball on the arm of Reese Carrington made my heart flutter.

"Go try it on!" Mom encouraged, ushering me towards the fitting room.

I must have tried on twenty dresses, none feeling quite right, before emerging in a strapless chiffon gown in a soft pink hue. My mom and Willow gasped.

"That's the one," Willow declared.

I turned and caught my reflection in the mirror, the skirt swirling gently around my feet. I imagined Reese's face when he saw me in it, his eyes lighting up. This was the perfect dress.

The ball was going to be magical. I just knew it.

As I peeled off my dress in the changing room, I could hear my mom's voice carrying on a conversation with someone on the phone.

"Cindee! It's so wonderful to hear your voice," Mom said, and I froze, recognizing the name. Boston's mom. "Yes, tonight's the big game, and I just wanted to make sure you're still coming. You know how much this means to him."

I leaned against the wall, peering around the curtain, watching as Mom's eyes closed briefly in what seemed like a silent prayer. Her fingers drummed lightly on the armrest, betraying her calm demeanor. Representatives from the MLB would be there, and we all knew a good performance could set his future ablaze with opportunities.

"Of course, I understand. It's quite the drive," Mom continued, nodding even though Ms. Riley couldn't see. "But you won't miss it. Oh, that's fantastic!"

The sigh of relief that Mom exhaled was palpable, and her shoulders relaxed. She caught sight of me peeking around the corner and waved me over with a bright smile, mouthing the words 'She's coming' with barely contained joy.

"Alright, dear. Drive safe, and see you soon. We'll save you a seat," Mom concluded, placing the phone back in her purse. She turned to me, excitement dancing in her eyes. "Cindee is on her way."

"Perfect," I breathed out, the nervous flutter in my stomach easing somewhat. I couldn't believe that she was actually going to make it to a summer game, and the most important one. For Boston, tonight would be unforgettable. And knowing that his mom would be there in the stands made my heart lighter, too. After all, no victory would taste as sweet without sharing it with those who cheered for you the loudest.

I sank into the plush velvet of the sofa. Across from me, my mom perched on an identical couch, her eyes were soft and brimming with unspoken thoughts.

"Chandler," she began, her voice carrying that maternal tone, "I was still a little taken back that you are going to this with Reese Carrington." She folded her hands in her lap, her wedding band catching the light. "He's not who I would have pictured you with."

I couldn't suppress the smirk tugging at the corners of my mouth. "Who did you picture me with, Mom? That tight end you love?" I raised an eyebrow playfully. "Pretty sure he's taken."

We shared a moment, a silent understanding knowing how much she always gushed over him. She had a tendency to only watch football when her favorite player was on the screen. Her lips twitched, fighting back a smile before she laughed. "Oh, Chandler," she said, shaking her head in amusement. "That would be a disaster. If you were with him, you would never get anything done around the house. You'd always be laughing."

I leaned back, my fingers tracing a pattern into the arm of the sofa. "Sounds like a divorce waiting to happen," I conceded with a half-smile.

"But seriously," she continued, her expression shifting to one of concern. "Reese has always caused some trouble. With Boston... and even Parker in the past."

I met her eyes steadily. "I know, Mom." My voice was firm. "But Reese—he's a lot different than he seems."

She sighed, a soft exhale of understanding. "I understand that, honey. Just... be careful, okay?" Her hand reached out, fingers brushing against mine in a fleeting gesture of caution.

Those words were becoming too familiar. "I will, Mom," I assured her, though the edges of my patience were beginning to fray. I was getting tired of people saying that to me. I was tired of the warning that hung over my head like a storm cloud.

A few hours later, the lights of the baseball field cut through the dusk, illuminating the neatly lined chalk and the crowd gathering in the stands. The energy was electric as players from both teams warmed up on the field, tossing balls back and forth to loosen up their arms.

"Chandler, look over there," my dad whispered, nudging me gently in the ribs with his elbow.

"Where?" I followed his gaze toward several people taking their seats.

"Guy in the red shirt, a couple rows behind us." He tilted his head slightly to direct my attention. "He's on the coaching staff for the Atlanta Braves."

I nodded, my stomach fluttering with excitement. The possibility that any of them could be one step closer to their dreams sent a surge of nervous energy through me.

My eyes found Boston in the dugout, laughing with some teammates. He seemed loose and relaxed, his blonde hair windswept as usual. Then I noticed Reese standing nearby, an intense look of focus on his face as he watched the players on the field. His jaw was clenched and his eyes blazed with competitive fire.

"Reese looks ready to dominate out there," I remarked.

Dad agreed. "Yeah, I'm sure they're all feeling the pressure."

I hoped they would shine under the stress and knew they all had what it took to play at the pro level. Win or lose, there's no way anyone could deny the talent on that team.

The announcer's voice boomed through the speakers, introducing the starting lineup. It was time. The boys jogged out onto the field, game faces on. I tilted my head, scanning the crowd for one person I really wanted to find. Just then, like a stroke of fate, Boston's mom weaved her way through the crowd, giving us a sense of relief. She slipped into the seat beside me, the space we'd been guarding with our lives.

"Made it," she breathed out, giving a faint smile as she settled in.

"Hi, Ms. Riley," I greeted, but my eyes darted to Boston, who just took his shortstop position. He looked in our direction, and for a split second, I could see his shoulders relax ever so slightly. Relief washed over his features—comforted by his mother's presence.

Reese stood on the mound, rubbing the baseball between his fingers.

"Think he's gonna throw a no-hitter today?" she asked, her voice quieter than usual, eyes glancing back and forth from Reese to Boston.

"Definitely," I replied, though I wondered why she was asking about Reese when tonight could easily be a huge game for Boston. Something else also tugged at my attention. Ms. Riley had always been the epitome of vibrancy, her cheers the loudest, her spirit infectious. Today, she was different. Her hair, usually flowing freely, was pulled back under a baseball cap.

"New hat?" I prodded gently, trying to gauge her mood.

"Oh, this?" She reached up, self-consciously touching the brim. "Yeah, just grabbed something on my way out."

"I have never seen you wear a hat," I teased.

She managed a half-smile instead, her eyes flickering away. "Thought I'd try something... low-key today."

"Low-key" wasn't a word in Ms. Riley's vocabulary, not when it came to supporting Boston. An uneasy feeling coiled in my stomach, but before I could inquire further, the umpire bellowed, "Play ball!" and the game snapped into motion. Ms. Riley clapped her hands, albeit softly, her eyes tracing every pitch and swing with an intensity that belied her subdued demeanor.

I watched her as much as I watched the game, and in those moments, the threads of worry began to weave a pattern I couldn't quite decipher. Something was off, but the why of it remained just beyond reach, hidden beneath the brim of a baseball cap and the forced curve of her smile.

Reese grinned as he took the mound and gave Parker a nod, his dark hair catching the sunlight as he turned. His athletic body tensed, preparing for the pitch. As his arm drew back, I noticed the pendant necklace he always wore glinted against his chest. With a sudden burst of speed, Reese's arm whipped forward, releasing the baseball in a blur. It rocketed through the air, cleaving a path straight towards home plate. Parker snapped his glove out and the ball smacked into the leather with a satisfying thwack.

"Can you believe that pitch?" I asked my parents, shaking my head in disbelief.

"Can't deny his talent," Mom agreed, her eyes sparkling with admiration.

"Wow," I breathed, unable to tear my eyes away from the next ball's trajectory. It was the fastest pitch I had ever seen, and it left me feeling more in awe of Reese than I had ever been before. The sheer power, the precision—it all added to his undeniable attractiveness.

As the game continued, I couldn't help but watch Reese with newfound appreciation. Each pitch, each swing of the bat—it all showcased his incredible talent. Whether he knew it or not, every move he made on that field only drew me closer to him, making it impossible to deny the growing attraction between us.

"Reese is really bringing the heat," my dad commented from next to me, his eyes tracking the game intently. "And Parker's got a cannon behind the plate. They make a good battery."

"Yeah," I agreed. "They're a great team."

I glanced at the guy in the red shirt, who looked impressed, before he whispered something to the person next to him. It was clear that he noticed Reese and Parker's chemistry, too. I wondered who else had caught his eye so far. If Reese kept this up, he'd certainly be on his radar, but I wasn't quite sure if Boston would make an impression tonight, and I knew how badly he deserved it.

"Strike three!" the umpire bellowed.

The crowd erupted into cheers as Reese pumped his fist. It was now the bottom of the third inning and Reese hadn't allowed any hits so far. I watched him walk back to the dugout, scanning the bleachers until his eyes landed on me, shortly before Blair caught his attention.

"Reese!" Blair called out, making him pause. "You got this!"

With a wink toward the bleachers, he disappeared into the dugout.

A pang of jealousy hit me as Blair flashed a smile and batted her long eyelashes at Reese. I scowled and turned away. There were more important things happening that I needed to focus on. I found myself leaning forward in anticipation once more as Boston stepped up to bat. My stomach churned. Boston had two balls caught already today. Another bad at-bat and his opportunity to be noticed could be toast.

The crack of the bat echoed through the stadium as Boston sent the ball sailing into the outfield. He took off and rounded first, then second. The crowd roared, urging him on. The third base coach was waving frantically, and Boston put on a final burst of speed, as he slid into third in a cloud of dust.

I looked over at the guy in the red shirt again. He sat up straighter and then typed something into his phone. I clenched my fists, heart pounding. His focused expression was intent on the game, jaw clenched. He lived for these moments.

The next batter made it on first, and Boston slid into home plate. The next few innings our team continued to shut down the batters and bring in a few more runs keeping us ahead. The crowd erupted into cheers after the final out was made in the last inning.

I joined in, clapping and hollering, but through the raucous celebration, one thing stood out to me—the silence that came from beside me. Ms. Riley's hands came together in a gentle clap, completely unlike her.

"They just won!" I shouted trying to lift her spirits.

She offered a weak smile, nodding appreciatively. "Yes, they did great," she whispered, her voice barely audible above the noise.

I frowned, watching her as she rose hurriedly, her movements edged with an eagerness to leave.

"Are you not going to wait for Boston?" I asked, surprised by her rush.

She glanced back, her eyes skirting mine. "I'll just wait for him by the car, honey. It's been a long day."

Her response felt like a brush-off, and my concern spiked as I watched her weave through the crowd, head down, her cap pulled lower.

I knew something was off but I still couldn't contain my excitement as I rushed from the stands onto the field. I ran straight to Parker and threw my arms around his neck. "You did it!" I squealed. Parker laughed and spun me around. I caught a glimpse of Boston jogging over, his wavy blonde hair damp with sweat. Letting go of Parker, I leapt at Boston, nearly knocking him over.

"Whoa there," he said, steadying himself. His icy blue eyes crinkled as he smiled down at me.

"I'm so proud of you!" I said.

For a moment, Boston held me tighter, his hand lingering at the small of my back as I melted into his gaze before the team engulfed us in a massive group hug, hollering and cheering.

As we pulled apart, Boston kept his eyes on me, like he wanted to say something more. But then the guys tackled him again, and the moment slipped away.

I felt a hand lightly grab mine which surprised me. I turned to find Reese's intense eyes burning into mine.

"Hey, you," he whispered, pulling me close as he swept me up into his strong arms. I could feel the energy radiating off him from the game mixed with his charm, and I knew that I was powerless against it.

"Well, well, looks like you've actually impressed me," I teased with a wink.

"Oh, I'm just getting started." His voice dropped into a low, seductive tone before he insisted we celebrate at his house tonight. "The team will be there and I want you there too," he added with a sly grin. How could I resist that smile?

"Of course!" I agreed, my mind still fluttering with excitement over the game. "I'll be there."

The team whooped and hollered, already heading for the parking lot. I walked between Parker and Boston, our arms linked together. I was still caught between the excitement of the win and the mystery of Ms. Riley's uncharacteristically muted behavior. By the time I reached the parking lot, I watched Boston greet her with an embrace beside her sedan under the dim glow of a streetlight.

"Mom, you sure you're okay?" Boston's voice carried across the quiet lot.

"Of course, sweetheart," she said, pulling back from the hug. "I'm so proud of you. You played phenomenal tonight."

"Thanks, Mom. Are you staying so we can celebrate?"

She patted his cheek affectionately, avoiding his gaze. "I wish I could, honey. It's going to be so late by the time I get home, and I've got work early tomorrow. You understand, right?"

Boston nodded, though his brow creased with the same concern I felt. "Yeah, I guess. Just... drive safe, okay?"

"Always do," she said, forcing a brighter tone. She opened her car door and slid inside before adding, "I'll call you tomorrow!"

With that, she started the engine and drove off into the night, leaving us all behind as if she couldn't get out of this town fast enough.

twenty-one

THE THUMPING BASS of the music hit me as soon as Willow and I walked through the front door. Willow's eyes widened as she turned to me. "I can't believe Boston came!" Her voice was filled with surprise.

"Really? He's here?" The thought of Reese and Boston being in the same place at the same time worried me, but after that game, I doubted anything could spoil today.

The sound of Boston's unmistakable laughter filled the air. He was standing next to Bailey and Crew, his athletic frame towered above most of the crowd. Those unmistakable bright eyes lit up the room.

"... and then coach said, 'If I find it in the locker room again, you'll each take turns wearing it to practice,' Crew finished telling his story, causing everyone around him to burst into laughter.

Willow and I exchanged amused glances before walking over to join the group. When Boston's gaze landed on me, his lips quirked up in a crooked smile.

"Hey," he said. "Parker kinda forced me to come."

"I'm glad you're here," I told him sincerely. "You deserve to celebrate too, you know."

Boston looked doubtful, but nodded and focused his attention back on his teammates.

As I weaved through the crowded house, I kept my eyes peeled for Reese. I finally spotted him holding court in the kitchen, surrounded by a group of people hanging on his every word. He was gesturing wildly, impressing them with a play-by-play of the game. His eyes were wide with excitement and laughter spilled freely from his lips.

When he noticed me, his entire face lit up. "There she is!"

He extracted himself from the crowd and strode toward me. His energy was infectious.

"I couldn't miss celebrating with you." I responded as my smile widened.

Reese grinned and slung an arm around my shoulders. "It definitely called for a celebration." His eyes were lit up as he looked down at me. "But the best part is having you here now."

Heat rushed to my cheeks at his words. Reese slowly guided me over to the large living room that had been turned into a makeshift dance floor. His strong hand was wrapped around mine as I breathed in his entrancing scent. The sweet melodies of a slow song swirled through the air, creating a special moment just for us.

"Dance with me," he whispered into my ear, his warm breath sending shivers down my neck as he pulled me closer to him.

"You dance?" I replied breathlessly, our bodies melding together as we swayed to the music. The warmth and hardness of his chest pressed against mine, providing an unexpected sense of safety and comfort. My hands instinctively moved to the nape of his neck, fingers tangled in his dark hair.

"Not really, but if it's an excuse to hold you close to me, then yes," Reese breathed, his voice low and seductive.

I chuckled softly, my cheeks flushing at the compliment. Yet, there was an undeniable connection between us, one that seemed to only grow stronger each moment I spent with him.

"I can't stop thinking about you," he said softly, his lips grazing my ear. "When we won, all I wanted to do was talk to you about it."

My heart stuttered in my chest. I didn't know how to respond, overwhelmed by his proximity and the sincerity in his voice. I simply laid my head on his shoulder, letting the music and his embrace speak for me.

Lost in the moment with Reese, his words were echoing in my mind, when suddenly Boston and Caroline slow dancing nearby came into focus. I felt a tiny flicker of jealousy as I took in Caroline's arms draped casually around Boston's neck, her cheek rested lightly against his chest.

It was then that I caught Boston's gaze flicker toward me. His expression was unreadable for a moment—a brief flash that could have been nothing or something else, something I didn't expect. I quickly averted my eyes, confused by his reaction. Boston was just my brother's best friend—that's all he wanted to be.

As we continued moving slowly on the dance floor, I couldn't resist the urge to sneak another look. This time, my breath quickened as my eyes locked with Boston's electric blue ones. His expression was more guarded now, but I detected a hint of something in his eyes again that took me by surprise. Was he jealous? "No, that was impossible... wasn't it?"

As the final notes of the song faded away, a couple of guys who approached Reese interrupted our intimate moment. "Hey, Reese! Long time no see, man!" one of them shouted over the music, clapping him on the back.

Boston gently disentangled himself from Caroline's embrace and whispered something in her ear. She turned to leave the dance floor, and he purposefully strode toward me.

"Can I borrow you for a minute? I was hoping we could talk outside, just the two of us," he asked, an earnest look in his eyes.

I hesitated, glancing back at Reese, who was now fully engaged in conversation with his old friends. Caroline stood across the room near her usual crowd, watching Boston closely.

"Sure," I replied, curiosity overtaking me. I allowed Boston to guide me through the crowd and out the back door.

We walked in silence for a minute as we moved away from the pulsing music. Finally, Boston stopped and turned to face me. His expression was serious, almost nervous.

"What's going on?" I asked. My heart was pounding, though I wasn't sure why.

Boston bit his nail before looking up at me. "This is going to sound crazy, but I kept the bracelet because that was the day I told myself you'd be my girlfriend one day," he confessed, his eyes searched mine. "You're who I want—I've always wanted you."

I stared at him in disbelief, my mind reeling. Boston had feelings for me? Where was this coming from? "What?"

"We've known each other forever, I know. I thought I was doing the right thing by trying not to cross any lines with you. Things were just too complicated. There was never a right time to tell you, but I can't just sit back anymore."

His words hit me like a train, at full force—completely unstoppable, ready to take out anything in its path.

I stepped back, shaking my head. "Are you kidding me? You wait until now to tell me this?" Anger simmered inside me. "You had so many chances, Boston. The day I asked you about the bracelet, you could have told me."

"I didn't know how to go about this. Your brother is my best friend. And your parents," he paused, raking his fingers through his hair, "they're like second parents to me."

"So now is the right time?" I interrupted, stepping closer. "That's not fair, Boston. You have never said anything, never even made me think you were interested. And now that I'm with Reese, now you decide to say something?"

He let out a long breath. "Do you think it's been easy for me? Seeing you with him?" His eyes narrowed. "The biggest dick on the planet." He shook his head. "He's always been an asshole to me for no reason."

I drew in a sharp breath, feeling the weight of his words. It was as if this version of Boston, vulnerable and raw, was someone I'd never really seen before, despite knowing him for as long as I have.

"I know he's a jerk," I admitted softly, finding the courage to meet his gaze. "But I do think that somewhere inside him, he wants to change, and at least he's honest." My words hung there, brittle and bold. "You haven't been."

"I don't want to talk about Reese," he spat out the name like it tasted sour. "It's not about him. It's—"

"How do I know it's not?" My hands flew up in frustration. "How can I trust that this isn't just some kind of competition to you?"

"Because it's you," he said fiercely, reaching for my hands. "You're not a game to me. Chandler, I stood in the back of every play. Sweaty and tired after games, I never missed one. I've always been your biggest fan."

"You went to my shows?" I whispered.

He nodded, which made my heart swell with such an intensity that it felt like it was going to burst—into a thousand tiny pieces.

"Back at school, it... it never seemed like you noticed me. There was always stunning girls around you when Parker would bring me around."

You think I didn't notice you?" His voice was gentle and full of emotion, something I had never heard from him before.

"No. Why would I?" I asked defensively, not wanting to believe his words.

"Chandler..." He sighed, shaking his head. "Those girls meant nothing to me. But you," he paused, his voice cracking with sincerity, "you're not just some girl to me. You're the girl—the one I've always wanted."

The earnestness in his voice caught me completely off guard. I could feel his words tugging at my heart, stirring up emotions that I couldn't even begin to comprehend. But part of me was also resisting, overwhelmed by this. It was all too much for me to process at that moment.

"Well, I don't know what to do with this right now." I crossed my arms, glaring at him. "I am starting to really like Reese. And it's really not fair that you'd do this now."

Boston opens his mouth, but I cut him off. "Don't. Just...don't." I turn and storm back into the party, fuming. I can't believe he waited until now, right when everything was going so well with Reese. What was he thinking? I have wanted to hear those words from him for so long, but why now?

"Damn you, Boston," I whispered, closing my eyes against the swell of emotions.

twenty-two

I STORMED BACK into the crowded house party, my shoes stomping angrily on the hardwood floors. The music was pulsing, bodies swaying, but I barely noticed it all as I scanned the rooms for Willow. I had to find her, to vent about what just happened with Boston.

Just as I rounded the corner to the kitchen, I overheard a familiar nasally voice that belonged to no other than Blair. "I just can't believe Reese asked her to the ball," she was saying to her friends. "Chandler is so not in our league—she's not even from Bayside. She doesn't deserve Reese's attention."

I froze, my face flushing hot with embarrassment and anger. Of course, she was talking shit about me. How could this night get any worse?

I spun on my heel, no longer in the mood to find Willow. I needed a drink. Several drinks. I pushed my way to the kitchen and grabbed a red solo cup, filling it to the brim with whatever cheap liquor I could find. I downed it fast, relishing the burn in my throat.

The night wore on, and the drinks kept coming. With each sip, my problems felt further away—Blair's cruelty, Boston's confession, the mess of emotions happening inside me.

"There you are," came a smooth voice behind me. I turned to find Reese, his green eyes full of concern. "Looks like you started the party without me."

Despite my drunken haze, his charm still made my heart flutter. "Oh, hey," I said, swaying a little.

"Whoa, take it easy." He grasped my shoulders to steady me. "I think you've had enough for tonight."

His strong hands felt comforting. I realized how much I had longed for him all evening. Reese had a way of making everything feel at ease.

"Let me take you home," he said gently. Though he was hosting this party, his only concern at that moment was me.

Reese guided me outside to his truck, his eyes burning with a mix of concern and amusement, keeping a secure arm around my waist. The fresh air started to clear my fuzzy head. We drove in silence as I rested my head on the window, watching the streetlights slide by.

"Are you sure you're okay?" he asked as we pulled away from the driveway. I could hear the slight worry in his voice, but his teasing smile told me that he wasn't too concerned about my well-being.

"Never better," I slurred, trying to sound confident and failing miserably. My gaze drifted over to Reese, and I couldn't help but stare. The warm light highlighted his handsome features, making him look even more gorgeous than usual. It just wasn't fair how perfect he was.

"Reese," I mumbled, my words thick with alcohol. "you know, it's not fair."

"What's not fair?" he asked, his eyes flicking towards me for a moment before returning to the road.

"Your face," I said with a hiccup, giggling at my own absurdity. "It's so... beautiful. You shouldn't be allowed to look like that."

He laughed, shaking his head. "Says the most beautiful girl I've ever seen," he replied. The sincerity in his voice almost caused my heart to stop beating. "And you complimenting me right now means you definitely had too much to drink tonight."

"You're right," I sighed, resting my head on the cool window once more. "I take it all back, I didn't really mean it."

"There's the Chandler I know," Reese chuckled, clearly enjoying my drunken ramblings.

As the truck came to a stop, I felt more dizzy from the buzz than I had before. Without waiting for assistance, I flung open the heavy door. Before I knew it, my foot slid on the unforgiving loose gravel. Balance betrayed me, and I slipped out, my knee striking the sharp stones below.

"Damn it, Chandler," Reese scolded. He appeared at my side, his eyes scanned me. "You should've waited for me. Hang on."

"I thought I had it," I mumbled, more embarrassed than hurt now.

With a shake of his head and a sigh, Reese reached into the truck bed and pulled out a small first aid kit—the kind you'd probably find tucked away somewhere in my mom's car, not the rugged truck of Reese Carrington. His fingers worked deftly, peeling open an antiseptic wipe with a practiced ease that seemed at odds with his tough exterior.

"Ouch," I winced as he dabbed gently at the cut.

"Sorry," he mumbled, his focus never leaving the task at hand. Once he was done, he placed on a bandaid with cartoon characters all over it. Reese's rough fingers were surprisingly gentle as he smoothed the strip over my wound.

I couldn't help but giggle at the sight, the irony too rich to ignore. "Kids bandaids, Reese? Really?"

"You never know when a pretty girl might fall and need them," he responded, the corner of his mouth quirking upward. It was a rare glimpse into the softer side of him that few got to see. Then he added, "But also, my little sister goes fishing with me sometimes. Gotta have them."

I lifted my gaze, and there it was—an unspoken desire in his eyes. They were burning with something more than just concern. He had a way of looking at me that made me feel truly noticed, something I had never experienced before.

At that moment, we weren't just two people sitting on the ground—we were the only two people in the world. My fingertips grazed the warm skin on his arm and the rich scent of his cologne filled my senses, intoxicating me further. And then he kissed me. His lips were soft and full, inviting me in to explore the hidden depths of him. The taste of mint lingered on his breath, mingling with the warmth of his embrace. Our tongues moved seamlessly together, the passion fueled by desire and longing. Every nerve in my body seemed to come alive, wanting him more than ever before.

Before I realized what I was doing, I had moved, my hands finding his chest for balance as I climbed onto him. My fingers found their way under the hem of his shirt, exploring the hard muscles of his chest. The gravel beneath us was forgotten as I straddled his lap, my heartbeat hammering in my ears. His kiss was addicting. My fingers tangled in his dark hair, pulling him closer, deeper.

I needed more, I wanted to explore all of him—to know every inch of him. Despite my uncertainty about being ready for sex, I couldn't resist pushing the boundaries with him. Maybe it was the alcohol, guiding me like a force beyond my control. My hand hovered over the button of his jeans, torn between desire and hesitation. But finally, I unbuttoned them slowly, my anticipation building with each passing moment.

"Chandler," he gasped against my lips, a mix of desire and restraint. Then he pulled away slightly as he bit his lip seductively, holding my gaze. "Listen, once you start fucking around with me, you won't be able to stop," he said, his tone filled with certainty. "You'll want it all the time. Trust me, it's a whole thing." He paused, tilting up his chin. "And I'm prepared for that, but you can't be under the influence when you decide to cross that line with me."

The air felt charged with electricity, each word hanging like a promise or maybe a very tempting challenge. I wanted to test that statement, to see if it held any truth, but I focused on keeping my breath steady despite how deeply intrigued I was by his words.

"Cocky much?" I shot back, arching an eyebrow to mask the effect he had on me.

"Don't you know me by now?" Reese asked, the half-smile returning, this time with a hint of mischief. "Only when I can back it up," he added smoothly, his confidence unfazed.

His assurance sent a shiver down my spine and the thoughts of what crossing that line with him might be like swirled in my mind. There was truth in his arrogance, a truth we both recognized, and it was impossible to ignore the allure of his audacity. His words held a weight that suggested he knew exactly what he was capable of—and so did I.

"And really, Reese?" I teased, lifting my knee to show off the Mickey Mouse bandaid he chose. "A Disney fan?"

A smirk played at the corner of his mouth, those dangerous green eyes twinkling with amusement. "Finding out new things about me every day, Chandler," he said, rising to stand in front of me before he helped me to the front door.

twenty-three

I CLUTCHED my throbbing head as I shuffled into the kitchen, the bright morning light like daggers in my eyes. Coffee. I needed coffee.

I filled a mug to the brim and took a long, scalding sip, leaning against the counter for support. The bitter liquid burned my tongue, but already my foggy mind felt a bit clearer.

The sound of footsteps made me look up. Boston walked in, his hair messy and his eyes were bloodshot. He gave me a hesitant smile. "Morning."

All of a sudden, it all rushed back to me. I replayed the events that happened last night—dancing with Reese, and the overwhelming jealousy that swallowed me whole when I saw Boston dancing with Caroline. Reese taking me home—and the embarrassing things I probably said.

"Shit," I groaned, rubbing my temples. The memory was vivid, as if it were happening all over again. I could almost hear Boston's voice, hesitant yet earnest, confessing something that seemed to tip my world on its side.

For years, I had imagined what those words would feel like coming from him—the boy who grew up tossing a baseball around next door. It was as if the universe had finally handed me a gift I had stopped believing I would ever receive. Little me, the girl who used to peek out of the window just to catch a glimpse of him, would be utterly beside herself. She'd be jumping on the bed, her pigtails bouncing, cheering at the top of her lungs because Boston—gorgeous, kind Boston—finally liked her back.

But it was just me, a much older me, trying to navigate feelings that were a complicated mix of past dreams and present realities. "Why when I'm finally moving on, finally happy, did he decide to throw a wrench in it all?"

Was it possible that Boston's feelings were genuine, untainted by rivalry? Or had I become just another prize to claim in their ongoing competition? Is this real, or is this just another game to him? Another competition with Reese?

"Great timing, Boston," I whispered to myself, resting a palm on the counter. "Really, just perfect."

He risked a glance my way, as he reached to grab a mug from the cabinet, trying to gauge my reaction. But I kept my expression carefully neutral, taking another sip of scalding coffee.

"About what I said..." he cleared his throat. "I had too much to drink. I shouldn't have blurted all that out." He stared at the coffee pot, unable to look me in the eyes. The silence stretched between us.

"Let's just forget about it, okay?" he said. "No hard feelings. I'm gonna give Caroline a chance and take her to the ball. She's excited about it."

"Sure, if that's what you want." I nodded, placing my cup on the countertop.

"So we're good?" he asked hopefully.

"Yeah. We're good," I replied evenly, turning my gaze away before he could see my expression.

Before the awkwardness could stretch any longer, we heard footsteps down the hallway. Parker emerged looking disheveled. His hair was sticking up at every angle. He squinted against the morning light streaming through the windows.

"Ugh," he groaned, making his way slowly to the fridge.

A giggle sounded behind him, and Willow followed him out from the hallway, wearing one of his t-shirts. Her blonde curls were a tangled mess. Boston and I exchanged a look, then burst out laughing.

"Well, well, look who finally got the girl," Boston teased Parker, who grinned sheepishly.

"What can I say? The Hartford charm runs deep," he joked back. Willow flushed pink but couldn't hide her smile.

I shook my head in amusement. "I am deeply, deeply disgusted. I don't know whether to be angry right now or excuse myself, so I can go puke in the bathroom."

The lighthearted moment made me temporarily forget about the awkward encounter with Boston. I was a little surprised, a little disturbed, but after the emotional roller coaster of last night, I was glad someone else had a good time.

"Let's have a little talk, friend," I said to Willow, which signaled to Parker and Boston that we needed to talk privately.

Parker and Boston headed toward the porch, leaving us to have a private moment.

"So..." I said, raising an eyebrow while glancing at Willow. "You and my brother, huh?"

Willow chuckled, her cheeks flushing pink. "Yeah, I know. It kinda just... happened."

twenty-four

I STARED at my reflection in the mirror, running my hands over the silky material of my gown. The light pink fabric hugged my waist before flowing out in layers of chiffon.

A knock at my bedroom door made me jump.

"Come in," I said, as I began to put my necklace on.

Parker stepped inside, decked out in a crisp black suit. "Wow, Chan. You look beautiful."

I smiled, though it didn't quite reach my eyes. "Thanks. You don't look so bad yourself."

I turned back to the mirror, applying another coat of lip gloss. "I know you're bummed about the game," I said gently. "You guys worked so hard this summer and deserved that championship. I know you didn't win, but I still think you guys are the best team."

"Yeah, maybe. But that's life sometimes. You give it your all and still come up short." He smiled ruefully as he began to lean against the door frame. "Now come on. One pity party is my limit for tonight. I still can't believe you're going to the ball with Reese Carrington. If only he knew what you looked like first thing in the morning."

"Very funny," I said, rolling my eyes and turning to face him.

Parker's playful grin didn't waver, but I could see the protective older brother lurking just beneath the surface. "And you going with Willow? Who would have thought we'd be here right now?"

"Never," he replied with a laugh. "I just hope I can make it through the night without coach benching me for next season since I'm taking his daughter."

Parker pushed off from the door frame and approached me, placing a reassuring hand on my shoulder. "Anyway, just be careful with Reese, okay? I've seen a different side of him this summer, I have to admit, but we're not like them. We didn't grow up here—with fancy boats and limitless credit cards."

"I'll be careful," I reassured him. "Besides, if things go south, I can always count on my big brother to save me, right?"

"Of course," he said, offering a gentle smile. "Unless I'm with a girl, then you're on your own."

I smiled and took one last deep breath before shutting the light off in my room. Parker's initial reaction when he found out about me going to the ball with Reese had been more shock than anger, which was a relief. I noticed Parker's perception of Reese gradually changing this summer. As his catcher, he had no choice but to build a connection with him.

As I took one final glance in the mirror, I couldn't help but feel a mix of excitement and nerves for the evening ahead.

"Boston already left to meet Caroline's parents before the ball," Parker said.

My smile faltered. "Oh. I was hoping to see him before he left."

Parker shrugged apologetically before stopping to take one last look at himself and fix his shirt in the hallway mirror. Sighing, I stepped onto the front porch to find Reese standing there holding the most gorgeous bouquet I had ever seen.

"Reese!" I said, surprised.

He looked so hot in a tailored suit that accentuated his strong broad shoulders and hugged his body in all the right places.

"Damn, Hartford... You look so good," Reese said, his voice low and husky as his eyes lingered down my body with an undeniable lust while handing me the bouquet. "And these are for you,"

I liked being the one who made his body stiffen, who made his eyes glaze over with desire. It was a thrilling feeling, knowing I could have such an effect on someone like him.

"Thank you," I replied, feeling my face get warm. "You don't look so bad yourself." He smiled, his eyes crinkling at the corners. That smile of his was lethal.

"Do a spin for me," he said, a playful grin on his lips.

Feeling slightly self-conscious but unable to resist his charm, I obliged. As I twirled around, the hem of my dress fanned out, creating a whirl of fabric. Reese's eyes followed every movement, taking me in as if he were trying to memorize every detail.

"Seeing that dress on you makes me want to take it off you," he whispered, reaching for my hand and placing a gentle kiss on my knuckles. His touch sent shivers down my spine.

"I know what you mean, that suit is doing something to me too," I grinned, a little shocked I said that out loud. Who am I?

"But too bad we have to get going," I said, eager to leave for the ball and finally get to see for myself if this event was going to live up to all the hype.

"Hey if you wanna get out of there and fog up some car windows—you just say the word," Reese said, winking flirtatiously.

I let out a laugh. "I'll keep that in mind."

He grinned, offering me his arm. "After you."

The past few weeks with Reese had been exhilarating. We had spent a lot of time on his boat, talking and laughing until sunset. We pulled pranks on his neighborhood watch—a sight that still made me laugh myself to sleep when I thought about it. Every day was a new adventure, drawing me deeper into his thrilling world.

At the same time, Boston and I had never felt further apart. I didn't know if that childhood crush would ever die but I still found myself wondering about him, and the things he opened up to me about. Lately, he was always busy, Probably with Caroline. It left an ache in my chest that I couldn't explain.

I knew he still had my friendship bracelet tied inside his glove that he took to every baseball game. But lately, it seemed like the only thing still tying us together was the past. We'd been like two ships passing in the night.

I was pulled from my thoughts as Parker suddenly appeared again, slightly out of breath.

"Hey, I put my flowers in the car and I'm about to take off," he said. "I know I convinced Coach to let me take Willow to the ball, but he wasn't too happy about it, and he'll kill me if I'm late."

I raised an eyebrow in disbelief. "Still not sure how you did it."

Parker gave a shrug. "I managed to persuade him after promising I'd organize the equipment."

"Nice," I smirked. "I'll see you there!"

Parker gave Reese a quick fist bump.

"See you at the ball, bro. Take good care of her," Parker said.

"You got it," Reese laughed, giving him a playful smile.

Parker grinned as he walked around to the driver's side of his truck. "Don't do anything I wouldn't do," he called out.

"That doesn't leave much." Reese shot back.

Parker just shook his head, chuckling as he turned the key in the ignition. The engine sputtered to life.

"Shall we?"

I took his hand, soaking in the feeling of his palm against mine. He led me down the steps to his shiny black truck, opening the door for me like a true gentleman.

The moment we stepped into the grand ballroom, I was in awe. Chandeliers glittered above us, illuminating the space in a warm, golden glow. White linen-draped tables were adorned with blue and white floral centerpieces.

But it wasn't just the lavish decor that surprised me. As we entered, all eyes turned our way. I felt my cheeks flush, unaccustomed to this kind of attention. Reese, however, was unfazed. He guided me forward with a reassuring hand on the small of my back, his charming smile easing my nerves.

"Don't worry about them, just focus on me," he said, low and calm. His eyes locked onto mine and I forgot about all the noise, getting lost in his mesmerizing green gaze. I wondered how he was hardly ever phased, even in the most intimidating surroundings.

We were interrupted by a voice calling Reese's name. A slender, youthful-looking blonde woman hurried over, throwing her arms around him in an enthusiastic hug.

"Reese! There you are! I've been calling you." she exclaimed.

He returned the hug warmly. "Sorry, I had it on silent. Mom, I'd like you to meet Chandler."

So this was Reese's stepmom. I had imagined someone older but her energy was infectious. She gave me the same warm, welcoming embrace that she gave Reese.

"It's so wonderful to finally meet you, Chandler! You can call me Britt," she said warmly. "Reese has told us all about you."

Before I could respond, a tall, clean-cut-looking man joined us. He greeted Reese with a firm handshake and clapped him on the back before he turned to face me.

"Chandler, right?" His handshake was firm, warm. "It's good to meet you," he said, his gaze holding mine for a beat longer than necessary, as if trying to read the story behind my eyes.

"Likewise, Mr. Carrington," I replied, feeling the weight of his assessment.

"Good to see you, son. Hope you're ready to claim your MVP title tonight." Though his tone was casual, I sensed an intense competitiveness behind the words. This must've been Reese's dad. It was clear that winning was important to him.

Reese's jaw tensed almost imperceptibly. "Guess we'll see what happens."

Reese's dad gave him a curious look, though the moment quickly passed.

Reese's hand found mine, his grip tight. I knew he was feeling the pressure, but I refused to let him feel it alone. Hand in hand, Reese and I walked through the crowd, mingling while his parents circulated separately.

I scanned the crowd, searching for a familiar face among the sea of people. That's when I spotted him—Boston, sitting at one of the tables with Caroline practically in his lap. He caught my gaze and shot me a playful wink before turning his attention back to the giggling girl beside him. He looked so handsome, but it was Boston, so I wouldn't expect anything less.

The announcer's booming voice came over the loudspeaker, welcoming us all to the ceremony, and asking us to take our seats. I leaned forward in anticipation, listening for what the announcer would say next.

Sure enough, when the announcer called out "Best Batting Average," Boston's name was announced and Reese rolled his eyes and let out an exaggerated yawn. I noticed the dismissive gesture and shot him a glare.

Boston walked up to the stage to claim his trophy, the crowd was cheering him on. He took a dramatic bow and I couldn't help but smile, proud of how far he had come. Something told me this wouldn't be the last of Boston's baseball accolades. I clapped loudly as Boston made his way off stage, trophy in hand. I knew how hard he had worked to earn that award. But the ceremony wasn't over yet.

"Next up," the announcer's voice said, "the award for Best Defensive Player of the season goes to "Parker Hartford!"

The cheers exploded all around me. Parker's grin was infectious as he accepted the award. I yelled, hoping he could hear how proud I was.

The ceremony seemed to be winding down, and I leaned back in my chair, thinking we'd seen the last of the accolades for the evening. That's when the announcement came that perked up every ear in attendance.

"Before we conclude tonight's celebration with the MVP award," the presenter announced, a hint of mystery lacing his tone, "We have our annual leadership award winner to announce. This next one is going to a player who is the voice of reason—someone who many look up to."

"Quiet down, I want to hear this," a voice whispered nearby, as everyone's focus returned to the announcer.

"The Christopher Michael Leadership award for excellent leadership goes to Crew Morrissey."

A loud applause erupted, the noise echoing off the walls, as players and staff stood to their feet. Crew, with his sun-bleached hair and bright smile, stepped forward from where he was seated. Reese couldn't help but smirk and cheer because Crew was his best friend.

"Way to go, Crew!" someone shouted amidst the clapping, and several whistles cut through the air.

"He's so dreamy," sighed one of the girls from the table next to ours.

"Total eff boy, unfortunately," her friend chimed in, leaning in closer as if sharing a secret. "I heard he was hooking up with someone in the bathroom earlier."

"Seriously?" the first girl gasped, her eyes growing wider.

Her friend confirmed with a knowing nod, her lips curling into a smirk that suggested she enjoyed the gossip as much as the news itself.

"And now, the moment you've all been waiting for," the announcer bellowed. "The Most Valuable Player for this season is... Reese Carrington!"

The crowd exploded as Reese stood up before jogging up on stage. I joined in the applause, extremely proud of him. As he accepted the MVP trophy, flashing his trademark smirk, I noticed Boston's smile fade ever so slightly. I knew Boston must've felt disappointed not to receive it, and I'm sure it stung a little that Reese got it.

But as the team came together on stage for one last team photo, I saw the two of them smiling together despite their rivalry. I let out a small sigh of relief. In the end, the game brought them together, even if only for a moment.

twenty-five

REESE'S ARMS wrapped around my waist, pulling me in close as we swayed to the music. I could feel his chiseled abs through his thin shirt, his muscular frame pressed against mine. Looking up into his eyes, I was mesmerized—I couldn't believe I was here with him. I had to stop myself from pinching my own arm to make sure I wasn't dreaming.

"You fit pretty well in my arms," he murmured, his voice low.

I felt a blush creep across my cheeks. "I like being in your arms," I replied coyly.

He grinned, his fingers trailing lightly up and down my back. I shivered at his touch, and my heart was racing. We held each other's gaze, the rest of the world fading away.

In this intimate moment, I was extremely aware of just how close we were. I could feel his breath tickling my ear, his body heat radiating into mine. I never wanted it to end.

"Chandler..." he began, his eyes searching mine.

My breath caught in my throat. "Yes?" I whispered.

He opened his mouth to continue, but suddenly a group of boys approached, eager to chat with him. Bringing us back to reality. The moment was over, leaving us both wanting more. He gave me an apologetic look before following them, his laughter fading into the pulsing music.

I sat at the nearest table, my eyes scanning the dance floor.

Moments later, Blair dropped into the seat beside me. Her red dress glittered under the lights as she tossed her hair over one shoulder. I wondered who her date was, or if she was important enough to get invited on her own.

"Hi. You're Chandler, right?" she said with a tight smile. "Having fun?"

I nodded, not wanting to make conversation with her, and glanced around for Reese. His teammates formed a circle around him, their boisterous laughter overpowering the music.

"So..." She traced her manicured nails over the white tablecloth. "You and Reese seem cozy tonight."

My cheeks grew warm as I thought back to how Reese was just holding me close during our dance, our bodies fitting together perfectly.

"Uh, yeah, I guess so," I said, fiddling with my necklace.

She let out a sharp laugh. "Oh, honey. You don't actually think he's into you, do you?"

I froze in silence as she smirked. I opened my mouth to respond, but no words came out.

Blair leaned in close, her floral perfume cloying. "Let me clue you in. Reese doesn't care about you." She examined her manicure. "You were just a pawn in his little game to get back at Boston. Trust me, long family history there. You might want to ask him about it."

Family history? I knew they had a rivalry, but what did it have to do with their families? She was probably just being spiteful, but I still wondered if her words had any truth to them.

I shook my head, willing the sting behind my eyes to disappear. "That's not true. You have no idea what is going on between Reese and I."

"Please." Blair rolled her eyes. "He's been using you this whole time. But I'm sure you'll figure that out soon enough. Just thought you should know."

With that, she pushed back her chair and then disappeared, leaving me alone with my swirling doubts. I sat there stunned, with her words echoing in my mind. Reese had been using me? Not the Reese I knew.

But the more I thought about it, the more I wondered. He picked fights with Boston at the games, and it always felt like his issue with Boston was something deeper than baseball.

Did Reese really care about me? Could I be a pawn in some twisted rivalry with Boston, a way for Reese to get under his skin? I felt the tears welling up as the thoughts sank in. Could I be that blind to Reese's manipulations? The seed of doubt that was growing inside me began to spiral out of control.

My hands trembled, and I quickly set down my glass before I dropped it. I couldn't stay here and let Blair think her words got to me. Pushing back my chair, I fled from the glittering ballroom, Reese's laughter was echoing in my ears.

I burst through the nearest door, gasping for air. The night sky enveloped me as I stumbled into the moonlit courtyard. My heart was pounding. Could he really do this to me?

Before I could spiral any further, the door creaked open behind me. I turned around to see Reese slipping outside, his brow furrowed with concern.

"There you are," he said softly. "I wondered where you went."

My hands balled into fists as he approached. "Don't come any closer. Just tell me the truth. Have you been using me this whole time to get to Boston?"

Reese froze, his eyes widening. For a long moment, he just gazed at me. His expression was unreadable. Finally, he sighed, running a hand through his dark hair. I took a step back from him, my heart pounding, aware of how the dying light made his features even more striking. The gravel crunched beneath my shoes, echoing the restlessness that churned inside me.

"It's complicated," he began slowly. "For a while, all I cared about was baseball and beating Boston, at everything. I didn't really have parents around, so I put all my focus into being the best. When I first talked to you, it was... it was just to piss him off. To get under Boston's skin," he confessed, and his gaze dropped to the ground as if the words were too heavy to uphold.

I recoiled as if struck. My worst thoughts were confirmed. Fresh tears sprang to my eyes. A part of me still felt like I didn't want to believe this even though I heard it from Blair and now I was hearing it straight from Reese.

"But the more time we spent together, the more I realized you weren't just some girl I could use to get to Boston," Reese continued urgently. "You're so much more than that, Chandler. You're smart and funny, and I ended up liking you more each time I was around you."

He took a tentative step toward me. "My feelings for you are real. Please believe that. It may have started over something stupid, but it didn't take long for me to see you. Really see you. The way your nose wrinkles when you laugh, like it's laughing along with us. And your eyes..." He reached out as if he wanted to touch my face but thought better of it, letting his hand fall back to his side. "You can see green and gold in your hazel eyes if you look closely. You're not like any of the other girls around here who always want something from me."

I blinked, unable to process his words and overwhelmed at the same time. My defenses wavered, wanting to believe him, to drown in the warmth I found in his gaze. I searched his face, looking for any hint of deception. But all I saw was sincerity in his features. I crossed my arms and turned away, fuming. Reese's words echoed in my ears, but I refused to acknowledge them.

"Why does getting to Boston matter so much? What family history do you have with him?" I asked, desperate to understand what this was all about.

"Who told you we had family history?" He said sharply, his eyes narrowing ever so slightly.

"It doesn't matter," I said cautiously, not sure what he would think about me hearing it from Blair.

His eyes clouded over. An impenetrable wall replaced the vulnerability he just displayed. "I—It's complicated," he said, frustrated. "There are things about my family, about my past with Boston, that I can't... I just can't share them with you. Not right now."

"You don't have to say anything else. I get it." I forced the words out, each syllable tasting more sour than the last. "It doesn't matter anymore. This," I said, motioning around us, "all of this started as a lie. And now everything else is tainted. Every talk, every kiss, every moment."

"Chandler, please just listen—" Reese started, reaching for my hand.

I pulled it back sharply. "Don't touch me," I hissed through gritted teeth. "I think you've said enough. It's sad because you ended up being the person everyone told me you would be and I really thought there was good in you. All signs pointed to "Chandler, don't do it"—and I did it anyway."

I started walking away when Boston suddenly appeared, his blue eyes blazing. He walked over to Reese, grabbing him roughly by the shirt collar.

"What the hell did you do?" Boston demanded.

Reese shoved him off, his temper flaring. "Back off, Riley. This is between me and her."

The two squared off, tension crackling. I could see their fists clenched and their jaws tightening. This was seconds away from a full-blown fight.

"Stop it!" I yelled, stepping between them. "Just stop."

The boys froze, breathing heavily. Boston's protective gaze found mine.

"Come on," he said quietly. "I'm taking you home."

twenty-six

I LET OUT a shaky breath as Boston gently took my hand, leading me away from the tense confrontation with Reese. My pulse was still racing from their near-fight. When we got back inside, I tried to hide my emotions as we walked through the crowd of people.

"Are you okay?" Boston's voice was soft and concerned. His eyes searched my face for any sign of distress. "Can you sit here for a few minutes? There's something I need to do."

"Sure," I replied, even though I wasn't sure if I was okay. He led me to a nearby chair, his protective nature radiating off of him.

"Wait here for me," he instructed with a small, reassuring smile.

I nodded, clutching my hands together in my lap as he turned away. That's when I saw Reese enter the ballroom, his presence commanding immediate attention. He scanned the room and for a moment; I thought he was searching for me. But before he saw me, Boston stepped into his path.

I couldn't make out their words, but their body language spoke volumes—it was clear they were arguing.

Despite being across the room, Reese's dismissive demeanor towards him was palpable. He maintained a relaxed posture, almost provocatively, as if he found Boston amusing.

"What are you talking about?" Boston's voice finally carried over, laced with frustration as he took a step closer to Reese, invading his space.

Reese's expression darkened. "I think you should be careful what you say to me," I could barely hear him say over the music. His eyes blazed with a sudden intensity. "Pretty sure you don't want me to go there."

I leaned forward slightly, my breath catching as I watched the intense exchange. Reese said something too quiet for me to catch. His lips barely moving, and then he leaned in, whispering into Boston's ear. The reaction was immediate and shocking.

Boston's face drained of color, his eyes narrowing in disbelief. For a moment, he simply stood there, frozen, a statue among the swirling dance of the ballroom. Confusion played across his features, quickly chased by a flash of anger and a shadow of shock, transforming his usually carefree expression into something dark and tumultuous.

Suddenly, it happened—a crack that tore through the room and halted the music as Boston's fist connected with Reese's face. The crowd gasped and recoiled as Reese staggered back, his composure slipping for a fraction of a moment. He tightened his jaw, and I saw the subtle tick that betrayed his effort to remain unfazed. Then, using his thumb, he brushed away blood from his lip. His expression morphed into one of dark amusement.

Before I could even process my next move, a voice broke through my shock.

"What the fuck, Chandler?" It was Parker. His eyes loomed over me, burning with anger and something else—disappointment. "Are you gonna date the whole fucking team or something? Just the infield or the outfield, too?" His words were sharp, cutting deeper than I expected.

"I don't need this shit right now, Parker," I snapped, my own anger flaring. "That's not what I'm trying to do."

"Sure looks like it from here," Parker shot back with a scowl, glancing over at the interaction.

"Move," I said sternly, as I shoved past Parker.

I saw that Boston stormed out—the door slamming behind him with a resounding echo that cut through the music and laughter. My heart raced, panic threading through my veins. What had Reese said to shatter Boston's composure?

I knew I had to go after him, rising from my seat, my gaze fixed on the imposing doors that had just swallowed him.

I sprinted after him. His long strides had already put him far ahead. "Boston!" I called out, my voice strained with concern. He didn't turn back, he didn't even falter. The broad set of his shoulders just tensed further, signaling a storm of emotions that I couldn't read from this distance.

He reached his truck and stopped after walking to the passenger side. The door creaked open under his hand, and for a fleeting moment, I caught a glimpse of his profile—those once bright blue eyes now seemed distant and clouded over. He tugged at his collar, then gestured for me to get in with his other hand.

"Will you just talk to me? What did he say?" I asked, finally coming to a stop by the car, trying to catch my breath and make sense of what was happening.

Boston shook his head, and the corner of his mouth twitched as if he was fighting back words or emotions, maybe both. "Just... get in, Chandler," he pointed, his voice hoarse.

The vulnerability in his tone struck me. This was not the happy, laid-back Boston I knew. He let out a long sigh, closing the door gently behind me before walking around to the driver's side. An unspoken turbulence hung between us, putting us in a strange unfamiliar territory.

"Fine." I huffed, slipping into the passenger seat, my mind racing with questions. "But you're going to tell me what's going on, Boston Riley. You can't shut me out."

Once Boston slid into the driver's seat beside me, a heavy silence filled the air. My thoughts were swirling as I replayed the disastrous events of the night. I wondered if Boston knew anything about the family history Blair brought up, but I knew both of us didn't feel like talking about it tonight. I felt so stupid for believing Reese actually cared about me.

Boston gripped the steering wheel with an intensity that was far from his usual easy going nature. His knuckles whitened with the effort, and every now and then, he would flex his fingers as if to remind them they were still alive. I wasn't sure who was more upset, me or him.

Boston kept sneaking occasional glances my way as he drove, but didn't say a word. The moonlight illuminated his face, and the streetlights flashed by in a blur. The low rumble of his truck's engine was the only sound breaking the heavy silence between us.

"Are you okay?" I asked, noting the stiffness in his shoulders. They rose and fell with a deep breath, showing the inner conflict he must have been feeling.

He didn't look at me, his eyes fixed on the road ahead, but I saw the way his jaw clenched, a muscle ticking in his cheek. "I'm fine," he said. The words were short and there was no mistaking it. Something was really wrong.

"Come on, Boston," I coaxed, hoping I could break through his walls. "Talk to me."

"He told me some bullshit lie. But that doesn't matter. I should be asking about you," a sigh escaped him, ruffling through his wavy hair as he glanced briefly in my direction before returning his gaze to the road. "I don't know what happened back there between you and him... But I swear, if Reese did anything to hurt you, I'll kick his ass."

I turned to look at him, taking in the tense set of his jaw, the anger simmering in his blue eyes. Sweet, protective Boston—the one I always wished would be my knight in shining armor, was now prepared to defend my honor. Yet, this moment didn't feel quite as I had always imagined it would.

"I think you already kicked his ass." I said, placing a gentle hand on his arm. "And don't worry about me. I just want to make sure you're okay. Is your hand okay?"

He nodded, exhaling slowly as some of the tension left his shoulders. We drove the rest of the way in a more comfortable silence. My heart ached, wishing things would have ended differently tonight. But some things just weren't meant to be.

Boston pulled up in front of the cabin, shifting the truck into park. He turned to look at me, his eyes gentle.

"Hey," he said softly. "Come here."

There was something about those words, "come here" that made my breath hitch. Before I could react, he reached out and pulled me into a hug. I melted against him, breathing in his familiar scent— something uniquely Boston. I felt safe as his powerful arms wrapped around me.

We stayed like that for a long moment, neither of us wanting to let go. Finally, Boston pulled back just enough to look into my eyes. His hand came up to tuck a strand of hair behind my ear, his fingers lingering on my cheek. I shivered, a fluttering started low in my belly. We were so close I could feel his breath and see the intensity in his eyes.

"You deserve so much better," he whispered. "I never wanted you to get caught up in all that."

My heart pounded as he leaned in, looking at me with his eyes hazy in a way he never had before. For a moment—just one brief heartbeat suspended in time—he leaned closer, so close I could almost count each one of his long perfect eyelashes. I could have sworn Boston Riley was about to kiss me, and every fantasy I'd ever imagined about this very moment flickered through my mind.

But then he pulled back, and I didn't feel his warmth anymore. It was torture, an undescribable agony, knowing that the one thing I'd been picturing for years was within reach for a moment and yet still so far away.

"I'm gonna head to the lake," he said abruptly, breaking the moment as he shoved the car door open. "Sit on the dock and clear my head for a while."

"Sure," I replied, my voice steadier than I felt, trying to shake off the way I was feeling.

I let myself out, and I started to follow the path towards the cabin.

"Hey." His voice halted me mid-stride, and I turned to find him looking back at me, an unreadable expression on his face. "You coming?"

The invitation hung there, unexpected but not unwelcome.

"Okay," I found myself saying before I could even consider it because I didn't want to be alone tonight.

He reached into the bed of his truck and pulled out a checkered blanket. "Here," he said simply, unfolding the fabric and placing it around me.

And just like that, we walked side by side, drawn together by something neither of us seemed to fully understand. But tonight, under the stars and surrounded by the lake, maybe we didn't need to.

We sat on the dock side by side, and I'm sure the view was beautiful but I wasn't looking at the lake. It was him I saw—the way the moonlight played across his features, the way there was always something comforting about him, even when he probably needed comforting too.

He must have sensed my stare because he turned toward me, his eyes meeting mine in a moment of silent understanding. Then, slowly, Boston draped an arm around my shoulders, drawing me into his embrace. I leaned into him, my head finding a natural resting place against his chest. His heartbeat was steady, a calming rhythm that somehow put me at ease.

We sat there, just watching the water together, letting the rest of the world fade away. There was no need for words; the silence spoke volumes. In his arms, I knew with absolute certainty—I had never felt as safe with anyone as I did right then with him.

twenty-seven

THE LONGEST WEEK of the summer flew by and after doing nothing but reading and laying out, I figured it was finally time to leave the cabin. I walked up the driveway to Willow's house. Red plastic cups and crumpled napkins littered the lawn while groups of kids laughed and chatted on the porch. I tossed my hair behind my shoulder and took a deep breath before stepping inside.

The air was hot and heavy with the smell of sweat and spilled beer. I wove my way through the crowded living room, scanning for familiar faces.

"Chandler!" Willow's voice rang out from the kitchen. She skipped over to me and squeezed me tightly. "You made it! Get yourself a drink and come hang. I haven't seen you since the ball. I'm excited to catch up with you!"

I followed her to the counter as she was throwing away bottles and helped myself to some punch. The sugary liquid courage eased my nerves. "Great party!"

Willow grinned. "Thanks! There's more people here than I hoped for, but word always gets around quickly in Bayside."

She tipped her cup towards me. "Jello shots are on the counter if you want one."

"Thanks," I said, grabbing a cup and throwing it back, relishing the sweet fruity taste.

Willow leaned against the counter, looking wistful. "Crazy how summer's already over. Are you excited for another school year?"

"I guess so. It'll be nice to get back in the swing of things," I admitted. "But I'll miss you."

Willow smiled and squeezed my arm. "You can't get rid of me that easily. I'll be texting you every chance I get and you're only a few hours away. I will definitely come visit."

I laughed. "You're right."

We clicked our cups together in a cheers before heading to the party, determined to make the most of my last night of summer before heading back home tomorrow.

Out back, there were several people that surrounded a game of beer pong while others lounged on the patio furniture. Shirtless guys horsed around, tossing a football. And there was Boston, leaning against the wall, red solo cup in hand, surrounded by a group of girls. His blue eyes looked glazed and his words slurred as he entertained his admirers. His hair was tousled and his eyes distant in a way I'd never seen before. Something about him seemed off.

"Chandler! Over here!" Willow's friend Paola waved at me from across the room. I gave Boston one last glance before making my way over to her. We chatted for a bit, but my eyes kept drifting back to Boston. He chugged his drink and then grabbed another.

I had known him for more years than I could count, but tonight I didn't recognize him. The last time I saw him was the night of the ball on the dock. I thought things were good between us but he's been avoiding me. I took a deep breath and headed his way—hoping maybe he'd let me in.

Before I could stop myself, I was pushing through the crowd toward him. "Boston!" I called out.

He turned, surprise flickering across his face. "Chandler! What's up?"

"I have hardly seen you this week," I said.

Boston shifted on his feet, glancing around uncomfortably. "Yeah, I have some of my own shit going on."

One of the girls draped herself over his shoulder. "Who's your friend, Boston?" she purred.

I frowned. But before I could say anything more, the girl next to Boston grabbed him and they disappeared into the crowd, leaving me standing there alone and confused. What was going on with him?

Later, I wandered back into the quieter kitchen for a break. And there was Reese, leaning casually against the counter, swirling a freshly made drink. Our eyes met.

"Hey," he said, sounding defeated. An awkward tension hung between us, and I still hadn't responded to his calls or texts since the ball. I shifted my weight, unsure of what to say. Reese took a sip of his drink.

"Some party, huh?" His signature smirk appeared, but it seemed half-hearted. I nodded mutely. I missed the excitement of what summer was supposed to be—easy, fun. Not this mess of complicated emotions. When others started to crowd into the kitchen, I slipped back into the crowd, more confused than ever. A part of me expected Reese to follow me, to demand we talk, but he didn't and I can't blame him. I had been avoiding him, but I wasn't in the mood to deal with any of that right now.

It wasn't until later that evening that I finally ran into Boston again. He sat sprawled on the patio couch as a girl giggled on his lap, her hands entwined in his shirt as if she were claiming territory, while two others sat by closely, their bodies pressed against his side, all of them wanting his attention. There was never a shortage of girls around here——throwing themselves at the players, hoping to catch their eye. Boston was basking in the attention and drunk—there was no mistaking the sloppiness of his movements or the way he laughed at their jokes that probably weren't even funny.

"Okay, that's enough," I said to myself, feeling a surge of frustration. I marched over, my resolve hardening with each step, and I reached out to grasp his arm. "Boston, we need to talk." I raised my voice over the girls he was with.

He blinked, his focus shifting as he tried to make sense of my presence. The girl on his lap pouted, "Hey! Where are you taking him?"

"He'll be right back," I shot back, not caring for the sharp glares the trio sent my way.

"Alright, alright," he relented, though he cast a regretful glance back at the girls as I led him away from the couch. They huffed in unison, their annoyance showing, but I didn't give them a second thought. Whatever was going on with Boston, whatever had driven him to this point, we were going to hash it out.

"Tell me what's going on with you," I demanded, the words punctuated by the pulsing music that I could still hear playing nearby.

Boston chuckled, a hollow sound that almost seemed forced. "You wouldn't want to know." His gaze flicked away, then back, in a challenge. "Last time I told you how I felt, you blew me off."

I stared at him, incredulous, and in a swift motion pulled the half-empty cup from his hand. The liquid sloshed over the sides, but I barely noticed. "I didn't blow you off," I countered, feeling an anger boil in my chest.

"Didn't you?" He arched an eyebrow. "Because I'm pretty sure that's exactly what you did."

"That's not what it was," I said, my voice softening despite myself. "I've been waiting to hear you say you liked me since I was five years old, Boston. I've always had this stupid crush on you. I always hoped— hoped so badly—you'd see me as more than just Parker's little sister."

His features softened too, the lines of tension easing as he took in my words. There was a vulnerability there that I'd never seen before, a raw honesty that made him seem less like the carefree athlete and more like the boy next door I grew up with.

"Well, look at that." Boston's voice had an edge of exasperation as he reached for the cup in my grasp. "You never said a word about how you felt, either." His hand closed over mine, skin warm against mine as he held it there for a moment.

Then he shook his head, tugging the cup free with an effortless pull. "Just leave me alone, okay? Let me deal with shit how I want." The warmth had vanished from his tone, replaced by a cold dismissal that stung worse than I expected.

"You don't have to deal with anything alone. I want to be there for you." I took a breath, hoping to persuade him. "Let's get out of here, and you can tell me what's going on."

For a split second, I thought I saw something vulnerable flash in his eyes, but it was gone as quickly as it had appeared. "Nah, I'm good," he replied with a casual shrug.

I hadn't expected him to push me away so easily, so effortlessly. He glanced around the backyard, his gaze flickered through the crowd. "Isn't Reese around here somewhere? Isn't that who you really want?"

The question stung with a bitterness that was unfamiliar coming from Boston.

"I didn't even think things with you were a possibility, and then you told me at the worst time." My voice sounded more desperate than I'd intended, but I needed him to hear me out.

"I'm not in the mood for these excuses tonight." He cut me off, and the blue in his eyes seemed to darken more with each word. "Just leave me alone."

"Fine," I whispered, stepping back as if his words had physically pushed me.

He turned away without looking back. The girls erupted into giggles and squeals as he approached, their arms reaching out to reclaim him. Boston slumped down between them, forcing a smile as he lifted his cup in a salute before downing its contents.

I stood there, watching, feeling like I was five years old again— on the outside, looking in. Except this time, I knew Boston wasn't going to come to my rescue with fireflies in the backyard. Those days were gone, and maybe the old Boston was gone too.

After a while, I noticed Boston drank more than he could handle and my gaze flickered around until it landed on Parker, who was chatting with a group of friends a few feet away. I called out, "Parker! A little help here!"

He excused himself and jogged over, concern etching his features as he took in the worry on my face. "What's going on?"

"He's had too much to drink," I said, looking over at Boston. "Can we get him home?"

He smiled and nodded his head. "You know I got him."

Parker's hands were steady as he looped one of Boston's arms over his shoulders, guiding him toward the car.

"Come on, buddy," Parker urged gently, but with an underlying firmness.

"Parker, don't be like that!" a girl near Boston chimed in, her words stretching out in an almost childish moan.

"Sorry, ladies," he said, his tone light but leaving no room for negotiation. "Funs over."

I trailed behind them, my arms crossed tightly over my chest. Any other night, I might have found myself rushing to help, but tonight... Tonight, I was too upset at Boston.

We didn't say a word the entire car ride to the cabin, and I just wanted this night to be over.

"Chandler, can you grab the door?" Parker called back to me, his voice pulling me from my thoughts as he helped Boston to the porch.

"Sure," I sighed, pushing the door open wider as they approached. Still not a word exchanged between Boston and me— my silence was a heavy reminder of whatever was going on between us.

Inside, Parker navigated the path to the couch with practiced ease, lowering Boston down onto the cushions. "There we go," he sighed, wiping his forehead with the back of his hand.

"Thanks, man," Boston slurred, barely awake.

"Water. Drink," Parker instructed, pressing a water bottle into Boston's hands before giving me a look that said 'he'll be okay.'

"Let's get you some aspirin too," I heard Parker continue, his tone patient but insistent.

I lingered on the threshold, the night air still clinging to my skin. My feet felt rooted to the spot as Parker tended to Boston, and without thinking, I turned back towards the porch.

My breath hitched. It was as though time stuttered, and for a heartbeat, everything stilled. There, under the glow of the porch light, my eyes locked onto something impossible. Was I seeing things? I blinked hard, trying to dispel the illusion, but when my vision cleared, it was still there. How is it possible?

twenty-eight

"CHAN?" I heard Parker yell out. "Everything alright out there?"

"Give me a second," I answered, my gaze transfixed. My heart raced, the revelation dawning on me, leaving me reeling.

"Is that...?" I whispered, my voice barely breaking the silence of the night.

The petals shimmered in a radiant shade of blue, rare and resplendent under the soft porch light. A few of my grandmas favorite flowers were in a white flower pot, its bloom a vibrant defiance against the dark. The sight of it transported me, as if my grandmother herself had brushed her fingers against the delicate petals. For the first time in seven years, I could feel her presence. It was overwhelming.

"Chandler, what is it?" Parker's voice came from behind me, but I could hardly move, let alone respond.

"Grandma used to grow these," I managed to say, my voice thick with emotion. "They're so rare..." I felt a tear trail down my cheek. It was beautiful—no, it was more than that; it was a visit from the past, a fleeting embrace from someone I'd lost who meant the world to me.

"Reese," I murmured, the realization hitting me like a gentle wave. Only Reese with his reckless determination could pull off something like this.

"Did you say Reese?" Parker asked, stepping up beside me, his gaze following mine.

I nodded, unable to take my eyes off the flower. "He remembered," I said, disbelief coloring my tone. "I told him once, about grandma's garden. About how much these flowers meant to her... to me."

"Wow," Parker exhaled, the word hanging between us. "That's... That's some gesture."

I sensed he didn't fully grasp the gravity of the moment.

"It is," I murmured, unable to tear my eyes away from it. It was stunning, overwhelming, and so intrinsically Reese.

"Definitely not your average apology," Parker commented, a soft chuckle in his voice. "I mean, it's kinda impressive."

"Can I borrow your car?" I asked.

His brow arched playfully, already knowing where I was going. Then he reached into the pocket of his jeans. In one smooth motion, he pulled out a set of keys and tossed them at me.

"Take care of Boston!" I yelled over the rain that had just started to pour.

I knew I had to go find Reese. When I got back to Willow's house, I asked around frantically until someone mentioned he walked down to the boat dock. The rain poured down in sheets as I ran to the dock, my shoes splashing through growing puddles. There was no thunder, no dramatic claps to emphasize my turmoil. Just the relentless patter of rain, soaking through my clothes, plastering my hair to my skull. It felt fitting, this shitstorm that seems to keep unraveling all around me.

"Reese!" I yelled, as I saw him sitting with his legs dangling over the churning waters below.

He turned, his eyes meeting mine, not clouded by the weather but by whatever was going through his mind. The sight of him, so deceptively calm in the middle of this storm, made me even more angry—I could no longer hold my composure.

My voice cut through the sound of the rain, sharp and accusing. "Can you just tell me why? Why did you use me to get to Boston? How did you even know it would get to him?"

Water dripped from the tips of his lashes, as he looked over at me. "I already told you—I saw the way he looked at you. I know that look," Reese said calmly, his voice barely rising above the din of the rainfall.

I frowned, tilting my head. "And what about us?" I demanded, the hurt evident in my tone. "Was everything just... just part of your plan?"

"I'm not answering that. You know everything between us was real." he shook his head, standing up slowly.

"It's not fair," I spat out, the words tumbling from my lips, heavy with the weight of betrayal. "For using me to get to Boston. For whatever he's going through right now because of you, for making me start to fall for you when you were the jerk everyone said you were this entire time!"

"Chandler," he began, rising to his feet, the rain pouring down on his face like tears he would never shed. But I wasn't finished. Not yet.

"Did you enjoy it?" I hurled the accusation, stepping closer, each word punctuated by the slap of water against the dock. "Manipulating me? Did you laugh about everything with your friends? Did you get what you wanted out of all this?"

"Of course not," Reese countered, his voice raised above the thrum of rainfall. He took a step toward me, hands outstretched, as if wanting to bridge the gap with more than just words. "It wasn't like that with you."

"Oh, I'm sure," I said sharply, holding up a hand, feeling the sting of raindrops against my palm. "How can I trust anything else you say?"

The rain couldn't even drown out my thoughts, ones I wished I could unhear. Reese Carrington could reach parts of me I thought were untouchable. No matter how much the universe didn't want us to be together, no matter how many people warned me that I couldn't trust him, a part of me still wanted him—so badly.

"Hear me out," he shouted back, his hair plastered to his forehead, drops clinging to his long lashes. "You matter to me. I know you feel it. Why does anything else matter?"

"Because it does," I muttered, folding my arms protectively across my chest.

"Chandler, I wish I could have begun things differently," he said, and maybe it was my name in his mouth that sounded like the sweetest melody, or the way his gaze softened when he said it. "I do, but I can't."

"You're right, you can't," I interrupted, as I took an involuntary step toward him. "And now I can't trust you and things are too complicated."

He matched my advance, closing the gap until we were just a breath apart. "I regret why I first approached you, not that I did. Because meeting you?" Reese's voice cracked, raw and earnest against the storm's howl. "It changed everything. You're the only girl that's ever consumed all of my thoughts. You're the only girl I think I've ever really cared about."

His words, sincere as they seemed, did little to persuade me. I refused to let him in again. The rain mingled with the heat of anger on my skin, but the warmth of something else, something that refused to be extinguished by rage or reason, flickered stubbornly within.

"Well, there's nothing you can do to make it right now," my voice trembled, betraying the churning mess of emotions I fought to keep at bay. "We can't undo any of it."

"No," he agreed, his jaw set, his eyes never leaving mine. "We can't. But I'd do it all over again knowing it would end like this if it meant that I still got to spend the summer with you."

The rain intensified, hitting the wooden planks of the dock with an unforgiving rhythm. "You think you can just walk into my life, mess up everything, and what? I'm supposed to be okay with it?" I hurled the words at Reese like daggers.

"Hartford," he said, his voice laced with that infuriating calm that always seemed to surround him. "I know I hurt you. I'm sorry. I never used to care about who I hurt—but for some reason, when it comes to you, I care about everything."

"Just stop," I pleaded, but it wasn't clear if I wanted him to stop talking or stop making my heart race despite my anger.

"Nah, can't do that." Reese closed the gap between us until I could feel the heat radiating from his body. "Because no matter how pissed you are, I still want you, and I know you still want me."

"Even now, you're doing it," I spat out, my voice nearly lost in the tumult. "Charming your way through this. It's maddening. Even when you make me so furious, you—you..." My voice faltered as his hands found my waist, pulling me against him, the world tilting dangerously.

"Even then," he whispered before his lips crashed onto mine.

My lips parted uncontrollably, granting him access. His mouth moved with a desperation that spoke of unspoken apologies and silent promises. My fingers tangled in his wet hair, my body clinging to his. The rain continued to fall, relentlessly, as if what was happening between us was fueled by the sky. The raindrops mingled with our kiss, sliding down our cheeks and onto our lips. I could taste the rain on his tongue, the bitterness of the argument still lingered but was quickly dissolving with each passing moment.

"Reese..." I clung to him, the coolness of the rain seeping into my flesh, but nothing compared to the heat that radiated from our entwined bodies. My heart pounded, echoing the rhythm of the rainfall, and despite the conflicting feelings of desire and frustration, I couldn't ignore how good this felt—even if it was wrong. Reese was either the best thing or the worst—I couldn't tell which.

"I like it when you moan my name," he said, his voice low.

"You're making this so much harder. I don't know how this can ever work," I confessed, my voice barely audible over the rain.

"Do you wanna get out of the rain?" the sound of water over-shadowed his question, slapping against the wooden pillars below.

"No," I whispered, looking up at him. "Don't stop kissing me."

He obeyed without hesitation. The strength of his arms pulled me in tight as he lowered himself onto the dock, the old wood shifting under his weight. There was a steadiness in him that blocked out the surrounding chaos, and as he pulled me on top of him, I clung to him as if it were my lifeline.

He groaned as I bent to kiss the raindrops from his collarbone, the taste of the storm mingling with the warmth of his flesh. "You're driving me crazy."

"What are you going to do about it?" I teased, my voice filled with desire.

"You have no idea what I could do to you," he said, his eyes darkening with hunger.

His grip on my waist tightened in response to every kiss I planted along the path of revealed skin.

"Reese," I breathed out, parting from the intoxicating embrace just long enough to glimpse those piercing eyes, "I—I've never..."

"Never what?" he asked, the rain trailing down his chiseled face.

"Never... had sex before," I confessed, my voice barely above the sound of the rain.

"Chandler," he said, his voice low and husky, sending a jolt through me. He leaned in, his forehead resting against mine, our breaths mingling. "We don't have to do anything you're not ready for."

But that response, his proximity, everything about him—made me consumed with want. The usual caution that guided my actions, that reminded me of who I was—safe. Used to being in her bubble, Chandler seemed to dissolve under his touch.

"Maybe I am ready," I whispered, as I tried to push away any thoughts of doubt or worry about what I was getting myself into—I couldn't let those thoughts talk me out of this.

"No, you're not ready for that, but tell me what you want—be real with me," his eyes were serious and his voice was calm.

"Just touch me," I managed to get out before kissing him again.

His hands explored every inch of me—from the curve of my breasts to the dip of my waist—each touch sent sparks flying along my nerves until they pooled in an intoxicating heat between my thighs.

"Wait," I gasped between kisses, my voice barely a whisper. "What if someone sees us?" A flicker of caution I was unable to silence.

He leaned back, his gaze locking with mine. The corners of his lips turned up in a mischievous smile. "Then we better give them a show," he teased, his hands, strong and assertive, wrapped around my waist, drawing me in until there was no space left for doubt or fear.

His fingers worked at the button of my jeans, popping it open with a soft click that seemed to echo in the stormy silence. The zip followed a whisper of sound drowned out by our heavy breaths. His thumb brushed over the cotton of my underwear, a teasing pressure that sent jolts of pleasure radiating through me. I arched into him, moaning his name, craving more of the exquisite torture.

"More," I gasped, the rain mingling with the heat flushing my cheeks.

He eased my jeans down, his fingers slipping beneath the edge of my underwear with a boldness that belied his usual playful smirk. One finger slid inside, and then another to find me slick and ready for him—drawing a sharp intake of breath from me. His thumb resumed its slow circles as he continued to kiss me—I was leaning against him, riddled with need.

"Fuck," he said, his voice thick with want as he watched me. "You're so beautiful like this, wet from the storm... and you're so wet for me."

"God, Reese..." My hands found his arms, feeling his muscles beneath my grip, as if he too were holding on for dear life. Every movement of his hand, every deliberate stroke, sent a cascade of sensations that echoed the relentless downpour around us.

"That's it, baby," he coaxed, as he continued working me.

"I don't want things to be complicated—I just want you," I moaned, feeling close to the edge.

"You can have whatever you want," he promised, his actions amplifying the words.

Our moans, intertwined with the rain's patter, created a symphony that filled the air. Each surge of pleasure brought me closer to the edge, and Reese, ever the conductor of my desires, played me like an instrument he knew all too well. I felt myself unraveling, my composure slipping away.

"Shit," I gasped, my voice barely above a breath, "you're... you're making it impossible to be mad at you."

"Good," he responded with that signature smirk of his. "Don't fight it."

The pressure was building and Reese's grip on me tightened, not just physically but emotionally too, as if he was determined to hold me together while simultaneously pulling me apart at the same time.

"Stay with me," Reese whispered against the curve of my neck, his breath hot on my skin. His words were more than a request. They were a lifeline as I felt the waves beginning to crash over me.

"Reese, I—I—" The rest of my sentence got lost in a moan as the tension spiraled, coiling tighter and tighter.

"That's it," he urged, his tone commanding yet laced with something soft and tender. "I've got you."

And with those three words, it sent me spiraling. The world was closing in on me with his arms securely around me and the overwhelming rush of release. I clung to him, nails digging into the warmth of his skin, as wave after wave of ecstasy tore through me, leaving me breathless and spent in the aftermath.

"That was so hot," Reese said softly, with a grin.

"Can't argue that," I whispered back, feeling like I could barely stand.

As we broke apart, panting and soaked to the bone, reality rushed back in like the water around our feet. "I leave tomorrow," I said weakly.

"I know," Reese said, his thumb tracing my jawline. "Let's not ruin the moment."

I couldn't help myself from asking, "But where do we go from here?"

The question hung between us with uncertainty.

"I don't know," he said gently. "But I have you right now, and that's what matters." And with that, he pulled me into his arms, the strength of his embrace shielding me from the relentless downpour.

I understood why it might have been so easy to fall under his spell, why once you started going down a path with him—there might not be a way to turn back. As much as I hated to admit it, the overwhelming desire I had for him consumed me.

"By the way," I kissed him on the cheek, "thank you for the gift."

"That was not easy to get," he said, his voice low and slightly amused. "But you're worth it."

At that moment, surrounded by his warmth, listening to the raindrops and racing heartbeats, everything felt perfect—impossibly, irrationally perfect. And although I knew that perfection was fleeting, I allowed myself to savor it, to hold on to it for just a little while longer.

twenty-nine

MY EYES FLUTTERED OPEN, but my heart immediately sank with the weight of the inevitable. Today was the day we had to pack up and leave the cabin—and head back to Stillwater. I pulled the covers over my head, wishing the morning away, not wanting the endless summer days to end.

I listened to the shuffle of feet on the wooden floorboards outside my room as Parker and Boston began their morning—like it was just another day. The scent of coffee made its way into my room, but it couldn't lure me out of bed—not today.

All I could think about was last night—the way it felt like Reese and I were the only two people in existence. I should have felt excited about getting back to school, about another new year, but my heart ached with uncertainty. Reese and I, whatever 'we' were, would now be separated by a relentless two plus hour drive. And then there was the argument with Boston last night—that was still on my mind.

When I finally got out of bed, Parker was putting away dishes. He raised an eyebrow when he saw me—contemplating something.

"Hey, Chan, do you ever look at me and wonder if we had our own language as babies? Before we could actually talk?"

I rolled my eyes, allowing a small smile to break through despite the bittersweet morning.

"No, Parker, I look at you and wonder how you made it to adulthood."

His laughter eased the tightness in my chest, just for a moment.

"Hey, where's Boston?" I asked, uncertain if he'd even want to speak to me.

"He left early," he said with a shrug, his attention returning to the dishes. "Said he had an errand to run or something."

"Well I guess I'll get started on packing then." I sighed.

The click of my suitcase's stubborn zipper made it all too real—the end of another summer. For a moment, I let my hand rest on the fabric, feeling the texture under my fingertips—a tactile goodbye to the place and the people that had transformed me. With a deep inhale, I hoisted the last piece of luggage, its weight a tangible reminder that we were officially driving back, there was no stopping it.

"Here we go," I whispered to myself, heading towards the front door, reluctantly rolling the suitcase behind me.

As I stepped onto the sun-drenched porch, he was standing there—leaning casually against the railing, almost looking exactly like he did the very first time I saw him at the clubhouse this summer. Only I saw him in an entirely different light now.

"Reese?" My voice broke the silence, and he lifted his gaze, those green eyes locking onto mine. They were usually the color of the foliage surrounding us—a vivid, living green, but today they seemed stormy, as if reflecting his mood.

"There's the girl I was looking for," He smiled, but it didn't reach his eyes.

"Didn't hear you pull up. Why didn't you let me know you were here?" I asked, setting down the suitcase with more force than necessary, a pang of irritation breaking through my confusion.

He looked away, watching a leaf twirl down from an overhanging branch, taking its time before landing softly on the ground. "Just needed a moment to think," he said finally, his voice a low drawl that usually made my heart race. But now it just sounded distant, detached even.

"Think?" The word hung between us, as heavy as the humid air. Reese had always been an enigma, a puzzle I thought I had all summer to solve. But as the seconds passed by, I realized that maybe some puzzles weren't meant to be completed. Not now, anyway.

Parker pulled his suitcase through the front door, making his way toward the car. He paused by Reese, who was still leaning against the porch railing.

"Hey bro," Parker greeted him.

"Hey," Reese pushed off from the rail with ease. "Let's run it back next summer? Except we win that championship game next time."

Parker grinned, his eyes lit up with confidence. "You got it," he agreed, pausing by the trunk of the car. "I'm gonna need the school year to recover from those fastballs, though."

Reese laughed, a sound I really started to adore this summer. "Nah, you're a legend—you killed it this summer."

"Speaking of legends," Parker added as he opened the truck before tossing in his luggage, "you took that right hook like a champ." His voice was light but there was a glint of respect in his eyes. "And Boston already left early this morning, so I guess there won't be any excitement before we go."

"Yeah, I know." Reese's expression didn't waver, but there was a subtle shift in his stance. "I saw him before he took off. And don't worry—no punches were thrown."

How did he catch Boston before he took off? Then it hit me, Reese must have been the errand that Boston had to make—but why would he go and see Reese?

"Ah gotcha," Parker nodded, tapping the roof of the car before heading back towards the cabin.

I leaned against the porch column, the wood rough beneath my palm. Something was off. His smile wasn't genuine, and his tone was different. Last night he was all charm and passion, and now... he's cold.

I saw Parker's trunk still open, waiting for my luggage—a jarring reminder of reality impatiently waiting. I glanced at the suitcase and then back at Reese, trying to read his expression.

"Anyway, what's going on?" I urged, attempting to keep my voice steady. I reached for the suitcase handle, but my hand hesitated, hoping for some sign from him, some indication that whatever thoughts were swirling in his head—he would share with me.

"Chandler..." Reese began, and I braced myself for the weight of his next words, ready to carry them with me along with my luggage, back to a place where summer seemed like a distant dream.

"Yes?" He didn't call me that often, a word I used to love on his lips when he would let it slip but now it was darkened by his energy. This didn't sound good.

His eyes, those deep pools of green that I'd found myself lost in time and again over the summer, met mine with a bittersweet intensity. "So," he began, his voice laced with sympathy, "This summer was amazing—more than amazing. I'm lucky you even gave me the time of day."

I felt my heart drop into my stomach. "Where is this going?" The question tumbled out, desperate to halt the impending words I sensed in his tone.

"Look," he continued, reaching for my hand. His touch, once electrifying, now felt like a goodbye. "I have a lot of shit I need to sort through here. You're going back to college, a couple of hours away and you should enjoy it."

"I can enjoy it and still be with you," I interjected, the hurt spilling over despite my efforts to hide my emotions.

"Nah, I'd be holding you back," he said, squeezing my hand before letting go as if releasing me with it. "I'm going to be wrapped up in baseball during the school year and I have some stuff to sort out. The last thing I want is you waiting around for me, trying to do the long-distance thing."

I swallowed, hoping he couldn't hear the sound of my heart cracking open in two. "Reese, don't do this." My plea was barely above a whisper, my voice breaking with the unspoken acknowledgment of him ending this, whatever this was. How could he do this after last night? Did it not mean anything to him?

His silhouette was framed by the daylight peaking through around him, the perfect picture of the untouchable boy I'd somehow touched—even if it was just for the summer. "I have to do this...I can't be selfish with you," he said, his gaze drifting to some far-off place. "But I need you to know that I care about you and that won't stop."

Each word was a hammer to my heart, chipping away at all the pieces until it was completely shattered. I fought to keep my face composed, to hold back my protest. But instead, I nodded, acknowledging his words. Something had changed between last night and now, and whatever it was, it had taken the Reese I knew with it.

"But last night, you were..." I paused, searching for the right word, "different."

"Different how?" His response was quick, too quick, and he averted his gaze, focusing on a point just over my shoulder.

"You were kind, sweet..." I trailed off, studying him. The way he held himself—shoulders tense, a forced casualness in his posture.

"So today, I'm what?" he pressed, his fingers drumming an impatient rhythm against the railing. There was a defensiveness in his stance that hadn't been there before.

"Closed off," I said softly. The air between us felt charged, the usual easy banter replaced by a strange tension.

"I'm not closed off, it's just the reality of the situation," Reese insisted, though the tight line of his mouth betrayed his words.

I thought I knew what heartbreak was. I had played characters —like Ophelia, and I had recited lines from many heartbroken damsels with a conviction that I believed I felt deep in my soul. In those moments on stage, I was convinced I felt their pain, that I understood how they felt. But standing here now, I was wrong——

none of those roles came close. Not even close. This was heartbreak.

"Just don't forget me, okay? I'm sure I'll be back next summer." I managed to say. But I wasn't sure about next summer—if Boston would invite me to stay again, or if I'd have something else going on. Hopefully, I'd at least be able to make it to some of Parker's games.

"I'll be waiting," he replied, his smile not quite believable.

I wanted him to stop me and tell me he changed his mind but he didn't. The heavy suitcase dragged behind me with a sound that seemed to echo the finality of my summer. Parker was already tossing the last bags into the trunk, cursing under his breath trying to make them fit.

"Need a hand with that?" Willow's voice broke through the calm as she tried to catch up with me, her smile was warm and comforting.

"Thanks, but I've got it," I said, mustering a smile for her.

"Are you sure?" Parker chimed in, straightening up and wiping his brow.

"I've got it," Reese assured them, grabbing my suitcase and closing the trunk with a thud.

Willow wrapped her arms around me in a hug that I needed more than she knew. "I can't believe you're leaving already," she murmured against my shoulder.

"I know, this summer flew by." My words were muffled in her hair. The scent of her strawberry shampoo was one more thing I'd miss.

Parker hugged Willow goodbye and promised to stay in touch and let her know when we arrived safely.

As we climbed into the car, my gaze flickered to the rear-view mirror where Reese stood with his hands buried deep in his pockets. He gave me a long lingering look, almost as if something unspoken passed between us—a silent conversation of what could have been.

"Take care, okay?" Willow said through the window.

"We will," I replied, though my attention never left Reese.

Parker revved the engine, and as we began to pull away, I watched them shrink into the distance. Reese, who just captured my heart and then crushed it, and Willow, the person who brought so much sunshine everywhere she went—they were the anchors of a summer I'd never forget.

"See you next summer," I whispered, though they couldn't hear me. It was a promise to myself more than anyone else. My fingers traced the outline of my phone in my pocket, the weight of Reese's words still hanging in the air.

"Chan," Parker glanced at me with concern, "You gonna be okay?"

"Of course," I lied, forcing a smile as I watched the outlines of Reese and Willow blur together until they were nothing more than specks in the rearview mirror. "Just going to miss this place, you know?"

"Oh, believe me, I know," Parker replied with a nod, his focus returning to the road ahead.

But he didn't get it. Not really. No one could understand the ache of leaving something—or someone—that had seeped into your very being. As the miles stretched out before us, my mind replayed every moment of the summer, each memory a bittersweet pang in my chest.

And with my heart torn by goodbyes and the uncertainty of when I would see or talk to Reese again, I began the countdown—days, hours, minutes—until I could hopefully return to the sun-soaked haven where everything had changed. Until then, I would cling to the hope that some connections, once built, could weather any season.

thirty

"HEY," Parker said, glancing over at me with that mischievous twinkle in his eye—one that usually preceded his infamous foot-in-mouth moments. "You didn't forget your pussy willow, did you?"

I snickered. "What the hell is wrong with you?" I shook my head. "Clearly, my parents are pulling a prank on me by claiming that you are my sibling."

Parker raised an eyebrow in genuine confusion as he glanced over at me, his hands still on the steering wheel. "What? I thought that's what it was called?"

The earnestness in his voice nearly had me bursting into laughter, but I held it in, shaking my head while reaching for the flower pot I placed in the back seat. "No, Parker, not even close," I said, trailing my finger over a delicate petal. "I'm hoping to be able to do something with the petals."

"My thing is baseball, not plants," he conceded with a good-natured shrug.

The road stretched endlessly before us, knowing we'd have a couple hours until we were back home. I glanced at Parker, his face concentrated on the road, hands still steady on the wheel.

"Shit!" Parker's sudden outburst almost made me jump out of my seat.

"What?" I asked, startled as I looked around to make sure we weren't about to get into an accident.

Parker blew out a frustrated breath. "The awards—Boston's and mine—we completely forgot to grab them, along with some gear I left behind. We need to pick them up before we leave town."

"Seriously?" I slouched in my seat, already feeling the pull of our impending ride home. "Fine," I sighed, sitting back up. "Let's make it quick."

He nodded, already veering off at the next exit, doubling back toward the clubhouse with an urgency.

"Come on," Parker said, as he cut the engine. "Might need an extra set of hands."

"Coming," I grumbled, pushing the door open and following him across the gravelly lot.

Parker led the way to the main office and then grabbed the shimmering awards waiting on the main desk just before picking up a bag of equipment below it.

"Just carry this one for me," Parker said, handing me Boston's award, which felt cool and a lot heavier than I expected.

"Got it," I said, balancing the trophy against my chest.

"Alright, let's hit the road for real this time," he said, his voice carrying a hint of amusement as we started to make our way back to the car.

"Great season, kids," Coach Levy's voice boomed from behind, startling us both. His smile softened the habitual sternness of his features, and he chuckled, a rare sound I don't think I heard once all summer. "You boys were a royal pain in my ass, but it was an honor to coach you."

"Wouldn't be a team without a little trouble, right?" Parker shot back, grinning as he shrugged his arms.

"Trouble? That's putting it lightly," Coach Levy said, his words were saturated with sarcasm.

"Hey, Coach," Parker began, curiosity lining his brow, "how did coach Ivy convince you to let Boston and me on the team this summer?"

"Actually, Parker," Coach Levy began, shifting his weight to lean against the edge of his cluttered desk, "It wasn't your coach who convinced me."

Parker's brow furrowed, confusion etched across his face. I paused, still holding Boston's trophy as I listened intently.

"Wait, if it wasn't coach, then who was it?" Parker questioned.

"Reese's mom gave me a call out of the blue," Coach Levy revealed with a nonchalant shrug, as though the admission held no significant consequence. "It was nice to hear from her. Haven't had the pleasure in years—since high school." He paused, a reflective silence filling the room before he continued. "She said she needed a favor. Told me there were two boys who were the best there is, and that they deserved to play for the Blue Devils. Figured if she was reaching out after all this time, it had to be worth it."

"Reese's mom?" I blurted out, unable to contain my surprise. The pieces didn't quite fit together in my mind. Reese's family dynamics were complicated at best, but this didn't make any sense.

I glanced at Parker, whose expression mirrored my own bewilderment, then back at Coach Levy. "But why would Reese's stepmom want Boston and Parker on the team?" The question tumbled out, driven by curiosity and an inexplicable sense of confusion.

"No, not his stepmother." Coach's voice interrupted my thoughts. His arms were casually folded across his chest as if he were discussing the weather and not about to drop a bombshell. "His real mom."

"There's a picture of us kids," Coach Levy said, as he gestured toward a well-worn photograph on the bulletin board hanging above his cluttered desk. "We were quite the bunch back in the day." His finger jabbed towards the sun-faded image, pointing out faces.

Parker leaned in, squinting at the picture. There were several other photos that surrounded it, but none were as captivating as this one. There, in the middle of a group of grinning teenagers, was Reese's dad—who looked the same, sporting the same rebellious smirk that Reese had.

"Wow, Mr. Carrington looks the same as he did back then," Parker remarked with a chuckle.

Coach Levy laughed, a deep rumbling sound. "Oh, you bet. And right there—" His finger shifted slightly to the left, hovering over a girl with bright eyes and an unmistakable smile. "That's Reese's mom, Cindee."

"What the fuck?" Parker breathed out, leaning closer until his nose was almost touching the wall. Sure enough, there was the undeniable resemblance—the same unmistakable sparkling eyes that Boston had.

"Yep, she was something else, always lighting up the room."

The room seemed to tilt on its axis, and I blinked at him, my mind scrambling to keep up. "Cindee?" I asked while it was still not clicking in my head.

"Yep," Coach confirmed with a nod, unaware he had just detonated a revelation that would change everything.

Parker's jaw clenched, his usual easy going demeanor replaced by a look of dawning realization. Coach Levy simply watched us, his expression unreadable. "Are we seeing this correctly?" Parker asked quietly, but I could barely hear him over the rush of blood in my ears.

I shook my head, trying to piece this all together. Cindee... I said the name again, a whisper that gradually grew into a scream of recognition inside my skull.

"Wait," I stammered, my heart pounding like it wanted to escape my chest. My eyes shot to Parker, then to his coach, as if I could demand him to make sense of this chaos. "Boston's mom is... Reese's mom? No fucking way."